SHADOW OF GRACE

A WILLOW GRACE FBI THRILLER
BOOK 1

WITHOUT WARRANT

LIQUID MIND PUBLISHING

Liquid Mind Publishing

WILLOW GRACE SERIES

Willow Grace FBI Thrillers

Shadow of Grace

Condition of Grace

Hunt for Grace

Time for Grace

Piece of Grace (coming soon)

1 KEVIN TALBOT

My LITTLE SISTER has been my whole world, and right now I have one job — keeping her safe.

She's the only thing I care about. The only thing I've cared about for as long as I can remember.

Megan's long blonde hair reaches her waist, the ringlets always tangled, leaves caught in the tangles. Milk chocolate eyes, big as a doe's. Cheeks that are round and rosy, and fingernails that are always caked in dirt from playing outside with the other children.

I haven't been the best big brother for the last seven years. I couldn't protect her when the people came for us, snatching us away from our mother. Because of that, we've been kept here in this compound, and I've never found a way out.

Until tonight.

I've fought to protect her, to make sure she has what she needs. But of course, she hasn't had everything she deserves. I am just a seventeen-year-old boy, and she's a ten-year-old girl, and we live in a world where other people hold all the power, where they're playing a game we don't even understand.

I've tried my best to figure out the rules, to stay one step ahead.

And finally, at long last, I made a move.

"Kev, I'm scared. It's so dark," Megan sobs, her voice a whimper in the wind.

It's September in Olympia, Washington. Where we are in relation to the capital, I'm not exactly sure, but I need to get us there. I know the property where we've been living for the last seven years is tucked away in the woods, deep in the forest. The only reason I know we are on the outskirts of Olympia is because the night we were taken, I saw signs on the highway. I memorized them because I knew something was very wrong. I knew we wouldn't be returning to our mom in Seattle. That night, in the big white van, Megan was sleeping, oblivious to the danger ahead, tucked under my arm, a flimsy wing of protection. It was all I could offer; I would have given her the world, even then.

I want to wrap her in my arms right now and carry her across these trails. I don't want her to slip and fall. But carrying her will slow us both down. Instead, I grip her hand tight.

"We've got this," I say. "We're going to be okay." My words, though, lift to the sky, floating away as fast as I say them. It's impossible to know if I can keep that promise. Will we be okay? For her, I pray we will.

"Where are we going, Kev?" she asks, her voice so soft, so scared.

It breaks my heart. I've never been one of those guys who was tough or ruthless. I've been a different kind of brave.

The silent type – I keep my head down. I watch, I listen, I do my best to take care of those I love. To take care of her.

"I know we're going to be okay because life's been so hard for so long, there has to be another way," I tell her. My words feel so stilted, so unsure, and I hate that about myself. I wish I was more confident.

"I will always trust you," she tells me.

Those five words buoy my heart in a way she doesn't understand.

Megan is stronger than me, I know that for certain. She's tough. The dirt in her nail beds prove it. She's got grit. That girl, she's got determination. I wish I were more like her.

It's so dark out, and my foot snags on a fallen branch. "Shit," I grunt under my breath. Megan tenses, and I know why. That word is forbidden. Just like so many others.

The last seven years of our life have been about following a doctrine that is heavy-handed and physically enforced. Children have no voice, especially not a voice that uses crude language. They say we live in harmony – but I know better. For men like Father Benjamin, harmony is another word for control.

"Sorry," I mutter.

"It's okay, Kevin, but it's so dark. My feet are so tired, and I'm–" Just then, behind us, I hear a snap. A branch breaking.

I tense, and Megan feels it, her body straightening like an arrow as she crouches closer to me. "Oh no," she whimpers. "Who's coming?"

"It's fine," I say, "Don't worry. Don't worry, Megan."

Maybe if I say it enough, I will believe it too. Because right now I don't believe it at all. My heart pounds. We still, our feet planted, not wanting to make a noise.

"I'm coming for you," a voice growls. "I know you're out here. You've always been trouble. But that's ending tonight." It's Earl Dawson.

My hands turn to fists as I realize who's come after us. Earl's always had it out for me, even though he's about my age, and we should be on the same team. Instead, he acts like my existence somehow disrupts his rise to power.

It's laughable. He has much more prestige here than I do. He is held in the good graces of Father Benjamin. The thing is though, in the society where we've been living, power is this intangible thing. It's constantly shifting, I've seen that. And I know he feels it too. At any moment, Benjamin could choose someone else to be his protege.

I'm almost eighteen. Maybe Earl is scared it's going to be me, the next one who will get on Benjamin's good side, or maybe he just knows I'm smarter than him, that while he was off lifting weights all those years while we were growing up, I was reading. I was learning about the world as best I could with the books I had available to me.

"Kevin!" Earl shouts. "You better stop, you piece of trash. Benjamin's orders."

At that, Megan starts to cry. "Go," I say, leaning down to her eye level. "Go deep in the woods."

"I don't want to leave you!" she cries, clinging to my hand.

"You'll never leave me," I promise. "My heart, it's your heart. You know that, Megs, you know that." I wish I had a flashlight so I could get another look in her eyes. Those eyes that belong to a wild animal, feral with a longing to be free. "Go," I whisper.

"You'll find me?"

"I'll always find you. I'll always be with you," I tell her, and she flings her arms around my waist as I hear Earl's calls for me grow louder, stronger, closer. Her tiny hands around my torso give me confidence to be brave. "I love you," I tell her.

And maybe that's not what most seventeen-year-old boys say in the dead of night to a little sister, but those boys don't know Megan. She is love. She is light.

"Go," I urge, and she runs. Her tiny feet, whispers in the night, her long cotton dress whipping behind her. I can't see her, but I feel her.

Earl calls my name, and a flashlight crosses my face. "You think you're so much smarter than me, don't you?"

"I don't think that at all," I tell him. "I think you're taking things out on me that I don't deserve."

"You can't just leave like this," he says. "I don't know who you think you are, but--"

I cut him off. "I'm just done with that place. With all of you. With Father Benjamin and his lies."

"Don't talk about him like that. He's more than a father to me."

I smirk, even though I shouldn't; his naivete knows no bounds. How can we grow up in the same place, yet see the world so differently? "Well, he's never dad to me," I say. "You can have him. I won't fight you."

Earl doesn't agree, and his eyes darken under the light of the moon. "You're coming back with me. Benjamin gave me orders. You belong at Harmony." He reaches for my arm, his strength undeniable, his grip fierce.

Maybe I shouldn't have spent so much time reading. Maybe I should have spent more time working the fields, gaining muscle instead of memory.

"I'm not going with you," I say, trying to fight back. But he has a good sixty pounds on me.

Earl growls. "I'm not going to make this easy." He pulls out a knife, pressing it to my neck.

"Get away from me." My words are tight and taut. Laced with fear and he feels it.

He laughs. "You're such a fool. Such a coward. Obsessed with your sister like a creep. She is nothing, she's just a girl."

"I don't care what you call me," I say. "I know exactly what I am, and I know what you are too."

He chuckles at that. "Do you now? How much do you know?"

I try to push at him. I shove him with my free hand, but he pushes me to the ground. I try to reach my fingers around his neck, but it's no use. "Get off me, you freak," he hisses as his knife blade pierces my side.

"I'm not playing games, and neither is Benjamin!" he shouts. "You belong at Harmony, and you're coming back now!"

I scramble away, my boots grinding against the dirt of the trail. I press my hands to the wound in my side, calling out in agony, hating the idea of Megan being close enough to hear this. To see me weak. I want her memory of me to be that of a brother who is strong.

"You're nothing," I hiss, rolling away from him, unable to stand. The pain in my side is blinding, and I struggle to find my footing.

Earl uses my weakness to grab me by the shoulders from behind, digging the knife into my back. I cry out this time, loud like an animal who knows he's been caught in a trap. Knowing he will never be free.

I roll on the ground, clutching at fallen leaves, ferns in the forest, mossy rocks, anything. It's no use. I'm crying out in pain, trying to dart away as fast as I can.

Earl laughs maniacally behind me. He's only twenty years old, a young man in so many ways. But his brutality makes him a beast. He will do anything Benjamin asks of him. And then he will take it one step further. I know he is capable of killing me.

"Benjamin will want us back alive!" I shout at him.

"But he doesn't have to know I couldn't find you." He laughs, clarifying that he has no intention of letting me live. "You don't deserve to come back. You aren't a real man; you never have been."

It's so dark out, and Earl's flashlight has fallen on the ground, but I'm still scrambling, desperate to get away. I wish I had it in my hand so I could see where I'm going.

Earl, though, knows exactly what he is doing. "Keep crawling like the pitiful animal you are," he taunts.

I don't know why he says this until it's too late, until I've crested the edge of the cliff, until he kicks me with his steel-toed boot, sending me over.

My body is suspended in air for just a moment. And in that moment, I see the life I could have had with Megan if we'd never been taken all those years ago.

But the sad truth is, life wouldn't have been any better. We would have still been captives, just a different sort.

As my body hits hard against the rocky ravine, I feel my bones break. The wounds where the knife dug into my flesh release the life within me. I close my eyes, wishing it all had ended differently.

Wishing the start would've been different, too.

I'm not going to have another chance.

My only solace, as I take my final breath, is that Megan will.

2 WILLOW GRACE

WALKING onto campus on the first day of a new school year always feels like a fresh start, and one I wholly embrace. It's one reason I love being a professor of psychology. Every September it's like flipping open a new blank page in a notebook. And that is something I am always slightly emotional about. Having the chance for a new beginning feels like a gift I never expected to receive.

The campus of Conifer College is busier than ever, and thankfully there is another day of sunshine for us to enjoy. Rain will be here soon enough, so I plan on basking in the blue sky as long as it's around. It's in the mid-sixties and the sun is out, and the trees have just begun to change color. Pine needles sprinkle the ground, but not like they will in another six weeks. The grass has all faded to brown because at a college like Conifer, wasting water on maintaining a green lawn is not something the student body would approve of. Everyone here is a bit more hippie than haute couture, and much more granola than avocado toast.

Over time, I have become more attuned to the inclinations of the students here. They are unique individuals who have found this college because they are looking for an experience slightly off the beaten path.

That's something we have in common. I don't want to be in a big city. I'm not looking for the limelight, rather a simple life where I can feel safe while doing work that will create change. It may be a quaint existence, but it's also a life of my choosing. That privilege feels like a gift I never saw coming. I've been given a second chance, one that on some days I don't feel I deserve.

I feel light as I walk through campus, heading to my office in the lecture hall of the psychology wing. The air is tinged with salt water, the shore of the inlet a mile away, accessible from the trails on campus.

I'm not tenured here yet, but I'm hoping I will be soon. I just had my thirty-fifth birthday, and while I'm not feeling old, the divide between me and my students is ever widening. My skinny jeans contrasting with their wide legged pants and their middle parts versus mine on the left side of my long brown hair.

Still, we have plenty in common. The eighteen to twenty-two-year-old undergrads who enroll in my classes are full of optimism, wanting to make the world a better place. I've worked hard to make my own life experience keep me from growing bitter. Instead, I'm ridiculously optimistic, probably to a fault.

"Hey, Ms. Grace." A familiar face greets me as I unlock my office door in the psych wing. The fluorescent lighting is jarringly dull, nothing like the sunshine outside. "I can't wait for class," Caroline Saunders says with a smile. "See you out at the trailhead?"

"Yep, in fifteen minutes," I say, glancing at the watch on my wrist. Instead of giving lectures in a classroom, we learn while we hike and enjoy nature. Unorthodox, but it keeps my demons at bay. The fresh air is my favorite escape.

"I hear a bunch of the newbies are complaining," she says. "I told them to pack their raincoats and maybe buy some new hiking boots."

"I'm glad they have you and your expertise, but today is supposed to be a beautiful day; the rain is forecast to arrive tomorrow," I tell her with a smile, then add, "And I'm glad you signed up for this course."

"Me too. Nothing like a new semester with a class about creepy cult brainwashing to get me in the scholarly spirit," she says with a laugh, waving goodbye.

She's one of my brightest students and was a light in my lectures last year. Conifer College does things slightly different from bigger universities. Instead of lecture halls filled with two-hundred students, we work in cohorts of twelve to fifteen learners in tight-knit groups. Because of this, we can dive into the material in a more intimate way, really examining what we're learning and why. It's what drew me to this place even though I had offers at bigger universities in Seattle and across the Pacific Northwest.

I wanted something different, so I did something different. I took a job here even though it's not as prestigious because I wanted to make an impact in a bigger way, even if it's on a smaller scale. And I like having a class load that isn't as demanding. It allows me to prioritize my private client work and the research I need to complete for my non-fiction books.

In my office, I drop off my computer bag and set down my thermos of coffee. Taking a deep breath, I look around. I use this space when working on a research paper or a new book about the psychology of cult behavior – my area of expertise. I have written two so far.

Besides that, I prefer to stay out of this tiny office; being confined in a box has always felt like a trigger. I pull up the blinds, wanting the sunlight to shine through. I crack open a window, wanting to bring the outdoors in.

A friend pokes his head in the door. "Hey, Willow," Malcolm Baldor says. "I was hoping to see you."

I smirk. "Oh yeah, why's that?"

Malcolm has been a professor of law at Conifer for about a decade. When I got the job here, he was someone I got along with, which is saying something. I don't do relationships. I prefer to keep my world as small as possible. But I make an exception for Malcolm. He has a good heart, that is clear from his work. Before Malcolm started teaching he did pro-bono cases no one else wanted to touch.

"So," he says. "I was wondering if you wanted to come to trivia night?"

I frown. "Tonight?"

"Yeah," he says with a chuckle. "A group of us are going to meet around six o'clock at the brewery downtown."

"I'm not sure I can make it," I say.

"Oh, why?" Malcolm laughs. "I know you have nothing going on. All you do is stay cooped up in that cabin in the middle of nowhere. You've never even invited me over! Come out, have a beer. The wings are good at this place."

"Oh, well, if the wings are good." I roll my eyes. I avoid crowds, but I am grateful for the invitation. I am a private person, but it means life can get a bit lonely. I appreciate Malcolm's attempt at getting me out of my comfort zone. It shows he cares.

"I hear Tracy from the math department is coming, and I know you guys always get along."

"Tracy? I don't know her."

Malcolm laughs. "Willow, she sat next to you at the in-service day last week."

I twist my lips, trying to place her. I can't. Makes me wonder if I have allowed the lens in which I experience the world to become too narrow, too focused.

"I'll think about it," I say, not totally ready to commit.

He grins. "I'll text you."

"Is that your way of saying you're going to bug me?" I laugh, grabbing my keys and walking to the door. I meet him in the hallway. "Do you have any classes this morning?" I ask him as I lock up my office.

He nods, "Yeah, I have one in a half an hour. What about you?"

"Yep, I'm headed there right now."

"Let me guess, you're making the students walk down to the ocean this morning?"

I smile, "Hey, it's day one, I always do that."

"Do you know you've gotten quite the reputation lately?"

"Have I?" I ask.

"Yeah, I heard a bunch of first years talking about how taking Grace's class means they need to get a credit card at REI for all the rain gear they need."

"Just because I teach all my classes outdoors doesn't mean they need to go into debt."

Malcolm laughs. "Well, they're probably already in debt considering tuition."

I smile, remembering how good it feels to laugh. "Hey, look, I'll meet you at the brewery tonight. I'm not trying to be a party pooper."

He grins. "Good, because you are always the best at trivia."

I chuckle. "Sure I am."

"You are! You always know the most weird, obscure shit. We need you on our team."

"Fine," I say with a grin. "I'll see you later."

As I walk to the trailhead, I try to focus on the hour in front of me. The meandering dirt path I take to meet my students is littered with fallen leaves and branches. Mossy rocks on either side of me guide the way, and pink fireweed flowers grow from the dark soil, pops of color and life. A few minutes of walking granted me clarity; I know how I want the class to go today.

The students who signed up for this course are invested in the material, and I don't want to let anybody down. They are gathered where I directed them to meet, and I count fourteen in all, a good number.

When I introduce myself, a tall guy in an orange beanie raises his hand. "So are all the classes outside?"

Caroline laughs. "I told you they were."

"Yes," I say with a smile. "I do things a little unorthodox, but isn't that Conifer College in a nutshell?"

There's a snickering of agreement. "Look, we're in a beautiful place, and we're all inside enough looking at our screens, so we're going to operate differently in this course. There's an online portal where we can post our notes and questions in a central hub, but most of our learning is going to be done through discussion. Oral tests and conversations instead of essays and Power Points."

"I like that," says a dark-haired student who introduces herself as Sarah. She has on overalls and a turtleneck, her round glasses accentuating her brown eyes. She appears eager to learn. Similar to Caroline. I am grateful to have a class of students who are ready to engage with the material.

"Good to hear that," I say. "Today, we're going to walk down to the beach. The trail is a four-mile loop, and as we're walking and talking, I encourage you to notice your surroundings, be aware of where we are, why we are, who we are. Look at the students in this group. We're going to be working together for the next semester, learning about things that maybe you've never considered before. Not just why people join a cult, but how."

"And you're an expert in that?" the orange beanie boy asks.

Sarah scoffs. "Haven't you read any of her books?"

Ignoring that comment, I answer for myself. "I've done plenty of research in the field, yes."

"I read your book," Sarah says.

"Which one?" Caroline asks.

"The latest," she replies. "Tending the Flock."

I smile. "Well, then you already have a basis of understanding for what we'll be discussing."

As we walk along the trail, I can feel a collective intake of breath, the inhale and exhale as everyone allows the fresh air to circle around them and lighten their step. The ferns are knee high, the earth damp, and the birds are chirping as they jump from branch to branch. Now that everyone appears more settled in their surroundings, I begin discussing Cult Psychology.

"So does anybody know how someone is conditioned into a cult? What are the methods of brainwashing?" I ask, broaching the subject we will discuss all semester.

Caroline is the first to jump in. "Isolation, monopolization."

"Good," I say. "Can you tell me more about isolation?"

Sarah speaks up. "Isolation is a critical part. Being cut off from family and friends and not hearing from anyone but the members of the cult."

"Very true. And the smaller your world becomes, the more reliant you are on the people who are experiencing the same things as you. Family and friends would no longer understand you because they haven't been through it." I look around at the students. "Any other ideas?"

"Exhaustion," another student adds. "Torture," says another.

"Exactly. You guys have good ideas, good instincts," I say, encouraging them, happy to see that the further we hike, the more relaxed everyone becomes. I see this happen every quarter – even the grumpy students engage the moment we are outside. "Here are some other ones too—how about hypnosis or enforcement of routine?"

"Drugs," says Beanie Boy.

"Yes, drugs for sure. All these methods create an abrupt, induced change and attitude. It reduces the subject's ability to think critically and independently, and that's when the introduction of new ideas and unwanted thoughts becomes more pronounced in their minds."

"What do you mean?" Sarah asks.

"Suddenly, the belief system you may have had, the values you once held dear, even your attitude about your place in this world, can change," I explain. "Isolation from your loved ones, from everyone you've known before, means a new culture is created. When your behavior isn't controlled entirely by you, you've been indoctrinated."

"Like if your beliefs begin to change, or if you're rewarded for your devotion, or if you're getting punished for thinking differently?" Caroline asks.

"Yes," I say, "all of those are signs you've been indoctrinated into a cult or otherwise dangerous group."

We've reached the beach by now, and we pause, staring out at the inlet. "Has everyone had a chance to walk down here?" I ask the class. Some of them nod.

"I'm a freshman," Sarah says. "I haven't been down this trail before, it's so pretty. I'm from Santa Fe, so we don't really get the water."

I look over my new group, marveling that I get to be here before them. "Then take it all in, really take it in, because this right here is life. And we are so lucky to be alive."

3 ROBERT HOWIE

As I SHOVE the last bite of maple glazed donut in my mouth, I think about how much of a damn cliché I am. But hell, I've never beaten around the bush about that. I've served as deputy sheriff for the last five years and spent my whole life in law enforcement here in Thurston County. This southernmost edge of the Puget Sound is in my blood as much as it is in my bones.

A call comes through the radio. And damn. It's the last thing I wanted to hear today. It's never easy getting a call like this, but when Cruz's voice comes through, I don't even want to sip my coffee. I just sit in my cruiser, taking in her words.

Officer Cruz is calling to let me know what a hiker has just reported. "A body's been found out past route marker 42, down the ravine," she says.

"Shit." I shake my head, starting the engine. "Dead on arrival?"

"Yeah," Cruz tells me through the radio. "A kid too."

"Shit," I say again. "How young?"

"Not sure. I'm headed out there now. Sheriff Moon is on his way over too."

"Roger that," I tell her. "See you in a minute."

Finally, I take a drink, the bitter coffee going down as painfully as the fact that the person found was a child. Of course, the death of anyone at any age is brutal. But there's something distinctly different about a case that involves someone who never had a chance to live their life.

As I drive through town towards the outskirts of Thurston County, I try to let shit go from last night, and instead focus on the moment, the present, the here and now. It's impossible though, because as I'm driving, my ex-wife calls, ready to give me another earful, laying in where we left off.

"I don't care if you have to work another shift," she says. "I need you there. He has a school conference, you know. You want me to do everything around here? I'm sick of it, Robert. Joint custody means you are around. But you're always MIA; I have no idea where you keep disappearing to!"

"I'm not disappearing anywhere," I tell Linda, but that isn't entirely true. More and more often I find myself on the backroads of the woods, needing space from reality. "Look, I know you're tired," I say, trying to keep my tone even. This woman has no idea the pressure I'm under, the stuff I'm going through at work. Sheriff Moon is a relentless hard ass. We don't see eye to eye on anything. With every case, we want to proceed differently. The tension it creates at the station is palpable.

Linda doesn't understand that. Or if she does, she doesn't care. Right now, she's concerned mostly about our son, who at fourteen years old is struggling in middle school.

There's a right to be worried. But hell, growing up is tough. And sometimes I'd just like her to let it alone a bit, let the kid be. Besides, the grades you get in eighth grade don't count for anything.

"I know what you're thinking," Linda says. "I can read your mind, Robert. I know you don't think it matters so much that he has a conference and that his grades aren't going well, but—"

"I *do* think it matters," I say, relenting, knowing that this fight is just going to drag on for the next week if I don't give in, give up. "Look," I say. "I'll be at the conference. What time is it at?"

"Four o'clock," she says. "At the middle school with his English teacher. Do you know who that is?"

I haven't a clue who that is, but I'm not going to tell her that. "I'll see you there," I say, ending the call before she can get in another word. We were married for five years too long. Got hitched because she got knocked up. And I know that's on me. My dad told me not to do it. My sister did too. I didn't listen. I was stubborn. Look where that got me.

As I pass mile marker 41, I'm on the lookout for where I should pull off to investigate the situation, wanting to let go of my personal life and instead focus on the job. Compartmentalizing is my mode of operation. Didn't say it was healthy, but it's working. Well, not for my marriage, but for the job, at least. I'm doing a fine-ass job here at work, and it's something I'm proud of. Probably prouder than I should be, considering my boss Sheriff Moon isn't exactly writing me any glowing performance reviews. You shouldn't always put work before your family. But then again, those people who say that haven't met Linda.

I pull up to the scene and see Sherriff Winston Moon's cruiser already there. Most people like him because he's good at putting on a smile, shaking hands, and getting reelected. Whereas I'm not so good at keeping my mouth shut.

I get out of my cruiser and look around. It's beautiful out here. Conifer trees as high as the sky. Cedars circling them. Sun-dappled trees that create shadows on the ground. I know this area well. The Pacific Northwest is a majestic place; these woods are one of the reasons I love living here. When work gets too hard, when life gets too complicated, hell, there's always another hike to find, an opportunity to get lost in my own thoughts.

I suppose that's why so many people out in Thurston County like living here. There's a comfort in the silence that nature brings. Of course, most people might not think that when they look at me. A mustache, a beard and a scowl usually line my face. But you don't have to be friendly to be a deputy sheriff. You just have to do a good job.

I walk to the body. Cruz and Moon are already there, along with a few EMTs. I kneel before the victim. He's not as young as I worried he might be. A teenager, nearly grown. "Any identification?" I ask Moon.

"None. But he has a few knife wounds," he says.

The shirt's been pulled back off the boy's torso. He's been stabbed in the side and the back. I shake my head. It's a brutal scene. His hip has been punctured by a stick, presumably on his way down the ravine. His legs are broken. "How long you think he's been out here?" I ask.

The EMT answers, "A day, tops."

I run a hand over my beard. "Foul play, obviously," I say, considering the wounds on his body are inconsistent with the manner of his death.

Sherriff Moon, though, frowns. "Eh, foul play? Who knows? This could have been any number of things."

I raise my eyebrows. "What number of things could lead this boy to being stabbed before he fell into a ravine? Or hell, was pushed, for that matter?"

"I don't know," he says calmly. "But we need to look beyond the facts of the case. We need to be sure before we make any unfair proclamation. Wouldn't you agree?"

He eyes me weirdly, and I know why. There's been plenty of times I jumped the gun. I level up to the worst-case scenario instead of taking in the evidence more thoroughly. Still, a kid wouldn't stab himself. In the back.

"Something happened here that's sketchy," I say. "I mean, a kid's been murdered."

"The coroner needs to rule that," Moon clarifies. "Again, we're not going to spread that around town just yet. All right? We need to ID this kid, and we need to build a case after scouring this property, these woods for miles. You understand?"

"I understand," I say, knowing he just put me in my place and not liking it one bit.

The body is placed on a stretcher and my stomach roils, thinking about the hiker who came upon this boy and had to report it to the cops. That kind of shit, hell, I don't wish it on anyone.

Back at the station, I run the prints. What I find shocks me.

"What is it?" Cruz asks.

I look at her. She's eager and interested in moving ahead in this department, and she deserves it. She's smart as a whip, less hotheaded than me and analytical. She thinks things through. It'll be an asset for her in her career. And she's still young, late twenties. Me? Middle of my forties, and I still haven't got shit figured out with my life.

"This kid was reported missing several years ago. Seven, actually."

"Seriously?" Cruz asks, shaking her head. "Damn. And that makes me think you got an age on the body."

"Seventeen."

Cruz runs a hand over the back of her neck. "That's so sad," she says.

"His name was Kevin Talbot."

"When he went missing seven years ago, was he alone?" Cruz asks.

"No, he wasn't," I tell her. "He had a younger sister, Megan. She would be ten now, if she is still alive."

I reach for my phone, knowing the investigation has now gone beyond local jurisdiction; the victim was also kidnapped as a child. I place the call, knowing the person I want to speak with is the FBI agent who dealt with the kidnapping case all those years ago. After looking it up, I learn the agent is Paxton Holt, and he is based out of the Seattle field office. He should have insight on Kevin Talbot, considering he is most familiar with the victim.

Once I explain the facts to Agent Holt, he requests the file as soon as possible. "I will be out as soon as I can manage," he tells me.

As I hang up, I see Sherriff Moon at my desk looking down at me. "What?" I ask, unable to tolerate his presence.

"Did you seriously just call in the FBI?"

"The ball's in motion," I tell him. "It's not like I can stop it now. And it's necessary. That's due process, Moon."

"You could have run it by me. I'm your boss, Howie."

"Sure, but I'm assigned to the case."

"Even so, calling the FBI without running it by your supervisor? I thought you knew better than that."

I shake my head, frustrated. "One day you want to hand things off to me and the next you want all control. I can't handle it, Moon."

He scoffs. "That's your job though, isn't it, Howie, to handle it? Even if you don't like it."

"Easy for you to say. You're the boss, right?" I stand up from my desk, needing another cup of coffee. Hell, a donut too. I didn't just find a dead kid today. I had to call the FBI. My boss is pissed. And I've got to go to a parent teacher conference with my ex-wife.

Not a good day. Maybe a second donut will help.

4 PAXTON HOLT

Back in my office, I can't help the smile that's spread across my face. Closing a case is always a satisfying feeling – and when the case involves a pedophile, it's even more rewarding.

My phone rings, and I move to answer it. It's Robert Howie, a deputy sheriff over in Thurston County.

"How can I help you?" I ask.

"I needed to call and let you know about a kidnapping case. It was one of your cases when you came to the bureau."

"Huh," I say, not expecting this. "You tracked me down about a kidnapping case from, what, several years ago?"

"That's the thing," Howie says, "it's not just a kidnapping case anymore. The person in question has been murdered. I ran the prints and got a name, traced him to you. I thought maybe you'd want to take a look at it, and maybe you could offer some insight, considering your previous involvement."

I grimace, hating that there has been a murder. Pulling a pen out of my shirt pocket and the small notepad I always carry, I focus on Howie's words. I flip open the spiral bound book to a fresh page. I always want a new start when I get a new case.

Howie continues speaking. "The name is Kevin Talbot. Does that ring a bell?"

The name makes me pause. I know that name. "Kevin Talbot," I repeat.

"Yeah," Howie says. "He's about seventeen years old, and he had two knife wounds, but he died due to a fall to the bottom of a ravine. A branch went through his torso. It was pretty..."

"Damn," I say under my breath. "Gruesome?"

"Yeah," Howie answers. "That's one way to put it. Of course, any case with a minor is difficult for those working on it, but I thought you might want to come out and be a part of the investigation. Take a stab at it. Pardon my language."

"I appreciate it. I do remember the Talbot case; it was so hard to leave alone, but there were no leads. They disappeared without a trace."

"It happens," Howie says. "The job can be a brutal one, right?"

Thinking of the case I'd just wrapped up, dealing with a pedophile – I know just how brutal this work can be. "Was Kevin alone?" My heart pounds at that. I remember looking at the pictures of Kevin and his little sister, Megan. Their mom was an addict and wildly distraught. When she finally realized her children were missing, she pleaded with us, desperate for help, for answers, and I worked my ass off trying to get them.

It's haunted me ever since that I couldn't find her children, her ten-year-old boy and her three-year-old girl, and now... damn. Her son is dead. "The little sister," I ask. "Was she found at the scene?"

"He was alone. There's no tracking, no footprints, at least none that we've seen. Although I have people scouting out the boundaries of the crime. A search party will start tomorrow. We need a lead. So far we haven't found anything to go off of, and no indication of his sister being with him at his time of death, or even where he came from and why."

"He didn't have any identification on him?" I ask, though knowing he was a minor, I'm not altogether surprised. Still, a driver's license would have helped.

"No, none at all. He wore very simple clothing, very rudimentary boots, rough haircut. He wasn't clean shaven. He seemed..."

"What?" I ask when Howie pauses.

"He seemed harmless is what I'm trying to say," Howie explains. "Weak, young, and now dead. So you remember him?"

"Yes," I say. "I do. Kevin was the kind of kid —from what his teacher reported and what his mom said — that would never hurt a fly. He was one of those boys who has a hard time in elementary school. He got bullied a lot, which made it even more heartbreaking that he was kidnapped the way he was. Gone from plain sight in a blink of an eye. He's the kind of kid you worry about, because..."

Howie clears his throat. "Because he doesn't seem like he'll stand much of a chance?"

"Exactly," I say, meaning it.

"Look," Howie says, "I'll send the file to your email. Is that good?"

"That's great," I say. "I appreciate it. And I'll be out to Thurston County soon to get to work."

"Great," Howie says. "And hey, whatever you did or didn't do seven years ago when you were trying to find this kid, don't beat yourself up about it."

I've never met Robert Howie before in my life. I know absolutely nothing about him, but he seems like he has his head on straight, even if he sounds a little rough around the edges. "I appreciate it," I say, not expecting this local deputy's kindness.

As I hang up, Kevin Talbot's name is on my mind, and even though Howie told me not to beat myself up about it right now, it's impossible not to.

If I had found Kevin all those years ago, he might still be alive.

A few minutes later I am called into Tamara Rodriguez's office. She's my supervisor, and the special agent in charge. She runs a sub office here in Seattle. Tamara doesn't pull any punches, and she always keeps me on my toes.

I'm not some beta guy, I'd like to think I'm an alpha, but I do like a woman who knows her shit. Tamara is one of them.

"I'm impressed, Paxton. You really came through on this case. And after so many other agencies failed to produce so much as a lead, I'm genuinely impressed."

I grin. "I've impressed you. I feel like I should be recording this moment," I say with a chuckle.

She rolls her eyes. "Don't let it go to your head." She is wildly confident in everything she does. Her power suits, her slicked back hair, her twin college aged daughters who are tennis prodigies, her husband who's a Pulitzer Prize winning poet laureate. I mean, for Christ's sake. This woman has her shit together, so to get praise from her in any form means something.

"Honestly," I tell her. "I appreciate the kudos. I don't exactly have many people in my life who know the ins and outs of what I do, and to hear you tell me I've done a good job means more than you know."

She purses her lips looking me up and down. I have no idea what she sees. She's fifty years old, as fly as J-Lo, and I must look like some punk to her. Fifteen years her junior with nowhere near as much experience.

"Honestly, Paxton," she says. "It's easy to dole out compliments when you do stuff like this, solving this case. I mean, hell, this stuff was complicated. This perpetrator was ruthless. He had so many victims." She shakes her head. Talking about the case is difficult for anyone, but now he's locked away for life.

"I hope I never have to deal with a case like that again," I tell her.

She exhales. "The thing is, Paxton, that's what this job is. It's always going to be difficult. No case is easy."

"Especially ones with kids," I say.

"That's true," she says. She glances over her shoulder at the silver framed picture on her bookshelf of her two daughters smiling on a tennis court. "I would do anything to keep those two safe. Maybe you'll know one day when you have kids."

Kids? I can't imagine it. I tell her as much.

"No?" she asks. "You're not interested in settling down, making a family of your own?"

"I'm kind of married to the job."

"Maybe find some balance."

I chuckle. "You're telling me to find some work life balance? Says the woman who is literally tethered to this desk fourteen hours a day."

"My kids are older, they're in college. It's different, but when I was young and your age, I don't know. I like to believe I had some sense of balance, but I also had a partner who was pretty good at holding down the fort."

"Your girls are lucky," I tell her. "A mom and a dad who stayed together after all this time. Successful jobs, creative and interesting and..."

"Okay, okay, why are you trying to butter me up so much?" she asks with a laugh, lowering herself into her chair behind her desk. She closes the folder she'd been looking at with details of the case I just closed and hands it to me.

"I'm not trying to butter you up," I say. "I'm mostly trying to get you to see me as the most essential FBI agent in the office."

"And why do you want me to see you like that?" she asks.

"Because you're my boss," I say with a laugh. "And whatever case comes in next, I'm hoping it'll be one I can get the chance to tackle."

"You confident you can handle a bigger case?" she asks me.

"Sure," I say, "I mean, I just caught this creep. I think I can handle pretty much anything."

"You've been here seven years, right?"

I nod. "Yep, just a little over."

"Where do you hope to go? Do you want to get transferred to a bigger office or..."

I shake my head. "I like Seattle enough. It's a mid-size field office. My cubicle isn't so bad."

She laughs. "Okay, so are you looking for a corner office? Because in that case, you're going to have to get a promotion one of these days. Is that what you're eyeing? *My* desk?"

I chuckle. "I don't want your chair, just a seat at the table, eventually. After I pay my dues."

"Good," she says. "That's what I like about you, Paxton. You don't beat around the bush. You know how to give a compliment, and yet your jaded edge makes you better at your job. You're not a rose-colored glasses kind of guy."

"Are any FBI agents?" I ask. "Because I haven't met one who wears their heart on their sleeve."

"I don't know," Tamara says. "Some agents view this job as their mission in life, right? To solve every crime, to put a bow on every case, wrap things up nice and tight, and there are others who..." I shake my head, not tracking. "There are others like you who don't just see it as a job, or as a mission. But who see it as a chance to make the world a better place. It's not about you as an officer, it's about doing your part for the greater good."

"You think I fall in the latter?"

"I like to think so."

"Maybe you don't know me as well as you think," I say with a laugh.

"Seven years is a long enough time to get to know someone," she insists.

"Is it now?" I joke.

"I'd say so."

"And what do you know?" I ask her.

"I know you put on a brave face, but underneath, maybe you're more of a softie than you want anyone to think."

"Is this your way of saying you want to send me on a blind date with one of your friends?"

She grins. "I'm not letting you date any of my friends."

"Why is that?" I ask.

"Because they are cougars," she said with a laugh, referencing her friends who were at least a decade older than me. " They bite, and I'm not sure you're ready to bleed."

I walk back to my cubicle, and my buddy Jedd looks over at me. "So did the boss give you a high five, a bonus, or a secret handshake into the mysterious club?"

"There's no handshake," I say, "but the club's pretty nice. It's down the hall. Just pass the filing cabinets, knock four times and ask for Peter Piper."

Jedd rolls his eyes. "You're such an ass."

I chuckle. But I don't disagree. I like to riff on this kid. He's new here, and he deserves it. He's a cocky bastard. Probably like I was fresh out of training. "No, but really? Did it go okay?" he asks.

I nod. "Yeah, it went pretty well. Maybe eventually I'll even get a promotion."

"You deserve it, man," he says, sitting back down in his chair.

My email pings, and I check my computer. The deputy sheriff in Thurston County got back to me with the case information.

I click it open, reading the names Kevin and Megan Talbot, feeling as if I've been pulled back in time to when I failed them both.

I was looking for a new case – and I feel like it has just landed in my lap.

5 WILLOW GRACE

THE TIRES on my old Volvo station wagon crunch across the gravel as I pull into my driveway. There's not a soul in sight, just how I like it.

After a long day on campus peopling, it's nice to have solitude. It's what I crave, even if it's something that scares me. It's what I know deep down in my bones. I'm a creature of habit, even if I've been trying to work through some of those tendencies for the last fifteen years. I lock the car even though I know no one is going to be coming down this mile-long driveway to rob me. Still, my instincts run deep.

I walk up to my front porch where two dark green Adirondack chairs face a small fruit orchard of apple and plum trees. My cabin is a tidy two-bedroom place custom built fifteen years ago. When I bought it, I was only the second owner, lucky to have so much established landscaping around the property. Wild mint and rosemary grow around the cabin, and there are plenty of seasonal wildflowers along with raised beds for spring planting. There is a covered well where I source all my water and a small garage adjacent to the cabin where I store my gardening supplies and yard tools.

After unlocking the front door, I check the trip wires and motion sensors. There is a control panel on the right side of the door, letting me see any comings and goings. I always take the same path to the cabin to avoid any monitors or alarm bells going off. I click through the screen to different cameras, double checking to make sure everything is enabled before I set down my things.

I'm not paranoid. I'm smart. There's a difference, even though many people wouldn't understand it. Maybe if they'd been through what I've been through, they would. Being able to protect myself is paramount. Everything else is secondary. I will not be at anyone's mercy ever again.

This is the way my mind works, and it keeps my world small and safe, a cocoon. I'm either at home or on campus. It's not because I'm not a people person, God knows I am, considering I went to trivia night tonight. I did plenty of smiling today, and that mask conceals my truth.

Still, every time I go out, I wonder if someone is watching, looking, waiting.

Tonight, though, at the bar, all was well. I had a pint of beer and a half a dozen hot wings. I answered a fair amount of the trivia questions and got along with the other faculty members who came out. I smiled and had fun.

It's not that I don't like people or public places, it's just it takes a lot out of me. After so many years of living a life that was so small, so sheltered, it's hard sometimes to do regular things. Small talk, grocery shopping, doctor appointments – they all require me to rally.

And that's after fifteen years of trying. I put myself through college and grad school and found a publisher after writing a book, really excelling in so many areas of my life. The areas I have a lot of control over, I manage well.

There are other aspects that are still so difficult for me to navigate, areas where I have to intentionally make a choice on a daily basis to be brave inside. My instinct is always to hide but being scared will never get me where I want to be. I want to learn to take risks with my life, but that seems like a long way off. Tonight, I will shower, make some tea, and do some reading. An introvert at heart, I need some recovery time.

I reach for the light switch, flicking it on. My cabin is illuminated. It is my sanctuary, and I feel so damn lucky to have a place of my own after living so many years where I shared literally everything.

I get a text from Malcolm. *Glad you could come out tonight, Willow. I know being social is hard for you, so I appreciate it. Plus, our team won! You can always come back out to trivia night next Thursday.*

I smile, typing back a reply. *I might just take you up on that.*

Really? He replies, quickly. *That would be awesome*!

Huh, I think. I wonder what I said that made him think my company is awesome. *Yeah?* I type back with a question mark.

You know I adore you, Willow.

I swallow, feeling like his words are more forward than I expected. I don't want to lead him on, and I am certainly in no position to date. *Well, I am glad we get to work together!*

I turn my phone to silent, setting it down on my coffee table. I sit down on my couch and tug off my shoes. My boots are dirty from being outside all day with the students. I smile as I remember their curiosity and their willingness to engage in the various lectures I gave. Three classes today, three hikes. It's a win overall. But my feet ache from walking, and I am glad to have tomorrow off.

I don't need to start a fire tonight. The warmth of September in the Pacific Northwest keeps the cabin a little toastier than I'd like, to be honest. I look out the window and see it has begun to lightly drizzle. Maybe the fire will be necessary tomorrow, depending on if this rainstorm picks up at all.

Since I already had dinner at the brewery, all I need is my nightly cup of chamomile tea after I take a shower. The hot water is glorious, and I stand under the shower head, letting the heat wash away the day. Once I'm cleaned up, I pull on sweatpants and a t-shirt, and then I make that tea.

Choosing a mug my co-worker Jay got me last year in the Secret Santa exchange, I fill it with hot water from the kettle. The mug has the words "Not A Hugger" printed on the side, along with the image of a cactus. I laughed when I opened it, realizing Jay knew me better than I thought. Getting too close to anyone feels like danger. A hug? Never.

Tea in hand, I walk to my work bag and pull out a file folder. While I spend most of my evenings preparing the lectures for my class or working on a new book, I have made an effort to give back. With my expertise in cult behavior and conditioning comes a wealth of knowledge, and I would be remiss to keep it all to myself. With the file open, I see the name Miriam Calloway, a 42-year-old woman who reached out to me after reading my latest book, asking for help.

As a professor of psychology specializing in cults and isms, I know a thing or two about cult survivors. I've been studying them my entire adult life. But Miriam Calloway wasn't studying them, she was living it. She'd just escaped a cult in South LA. This one wasn't about religion or an end of the world prophecy, instead it centered on wellness, masking self-help for mind control. Miriam gave the group her life savings, her home, her grandmother's wedding ring, everything she had. The fact she got out at all is a testament to her strength.

I flip through the pages of the file. We're having our first consultation in a few weeks. She wants to understand why she was lured into such a life. The thing I always try to emphasize when I talk to a cult survivor is that they're not fools. They're not stupid. In fact, they're brave.

They held so much hope that they were willing to risk it all. Most people aren't like that. Most people are too scared to go after what they want. The sad fact for survivors of cults is what they have gone after is something that eventually hurt them. I'm not sure exactly what I can say to Miriam to console her, but it's not about me. When we have our video consultation, the focus will be on her, on what she needs.

I'll do my best to guide her to an understanding that she has nothing to apologize for. She's not to blame. She was a victim.

And she's not the only one.

6 PAXTON HOLT

As soon as I finish reading the electronic case file that Deputy Sheriff Robert Howie sent me, I know I need to get to Thurston County. Now.

The report horrifically depicts Kevin Talbot's death . His body was brutalized and misshapen, a soul gone before its time. I know I'm not supposed to be sentimental about shit like this. It's a job, right? But maybe my boss is right.

Maybe Tamara knew what she was saying when she told me it's not about the job so much as it is about making the world a better place. And sure, that might sound cheesy, but I don't think I care. The kid is dead. This kid with a sister and a mom and a whole life that was taken from him before his time.

This can't wait.

I call Robert Howie and let him know my plans. "I'm coming over now." I tell him I will be there in a little over an hour, and he texts me a pin to where we should meet.

I gather my things and get in my car, then swing by Starbucks on my way out of town like a real Seattleite. Guzzling my Americano as I get on I-5 South to Olympia, I try to think about who would have it out for a kid and why. What I know from my field experience is that there's not always a clear motive. Some people are simply sick. Out of the gates, they were ready for destruction. So maybe it was a dangerous person who took those two kids seven years ago. But maybe there is a stronger motive, one that has yet to be uncovered. I intend to find out.

When I pull into Thurston County, I head straight to the location where Robert Howie told me to meet him. I see his police cruiser waiting for me at mile marker 42. I've never met the guy before, but he looks like he's had a rough go of things. Dark circles under his eyes, looking at his phone, and eating French fries out of a paper bag.

I want to give the deputy the benefit of the doubt. It's six o'clock in the evening, and maybe he's ready to be done for the day. I give myself a reminder to thank him for being accommodating. I reach out my hand in greeting.

"Good to meet you," I say. "I'm Paxton Holt."

"Robert Howie," he says gruffly. Then he pulls back his hand and runs it over his beard. He looks aged, weathered.

I wonder what he sees when he looks at me. A guy who's probably too cocky for his own good, who was blessed with athletic good looks and an easy enough disposition. But the deeper you look, the more you see I'm not charming so much as I'm determined. And the truth is, I'll put on the charm if it means I get what I want. Right now, I want Robert Howie's cooperation.

"I appreciate you meeting me here. I know it's late," I say, lifting my eyes to the sky. "And starting to rain."

"Brutal, right? Now that it's started, I bet it rains for the next six months," Howie says with a chuckle. There's a slow soft trickle, and I zip up my raincoat to my chin. He has done the same, and his wide-brimmed cap keeps his head dry. I pull my hood into place.

"Well," I say, "like I said, I appreciate you meeting me. I'm sure you have other places to be."

He grunts. "Just came from my kid's school conference. It was a hellscape, if you ask me. Never have children," he says.

"That bad?" I ask, thinking how Tamara was literally giving me the opposite advice earlier this afternoon.

He cocks his brow. "I mean, I love Joey to death, sure. But middle school is ruthless and that kid, hell, he's made it his life mission to piss me and his mother off."

"Sorry to hear that," I say. "Is he anything like you were when you were a kid?"

Howie looks over, giving me a sidelong glance, and he laughs heartily. "Hell, you got me there. Actually, you know, I'm probably still more like him than I'd like to admit."

"Good to know," I say jokingly. "So you're a bit of an asshole too?"

"Don't tell my boss." Howie chuckles.

"Oh, if you're an asshole, I'm sure he already knows."

Immediately I feel the energy shift between us. Howie is not my enemy, and I'm not his. He's an easy enough going lawman, and as he lays out the crime scene, I can tell he knows his stuff.

"It's pretty deep in the woods back here," I say, after we've walked a quarter of a mile from where we parked our cars.

“We were lucky there was a hiker out here at all, especially this time of year."

"It's just September, though," I say. "The weather's mostly good."

At that, the rain begins to pour more heavily on us.

"Usually, yeah. It's more that this just isn't a popular area for anyone to go hiking. The trails aren't maintained. No one comes out here. Still I'm thankful on the kid's behalf."

"For Kevin?" I ask.

He nods. "Yeah. You never met him, obviously. You only knew him as a missing person, right?”

“Right, him and his sister Megan were kidnapped. It was why the FBI got involved. But the leads were all dead ends – no one had any information. It was brutal. She was only three at the time. Now she'd be ten years old."

Howie nods. "Would love to know what happened to her."

"Well, I intend to find out," I tell him.

"That's good to hear because shit going down like this in this county, it's bad."

"What do you mean by that?"

"Well, it's the capital, right? We don't want too much bad press."

"I can understand that; it's a much smaller city than Seattle," I say, stating the obvious.

"Sure, but Olympia has its seedy pockets same as a metropolis like Seattle does. The homeless population has been growing and so has the income disparity across the entire county. People who used to make ends meet are struggling even while holding a few jobs. Families are moving in together to make things work. You know what I mean?"

I nod. "I do, and not just from reading about it in the paper," I tell him. "Growing up, things were rough for me. I got lucky enough to turn my life around."

Howie nods. "I guess the bureau takes all kinds, huh?"

I shrug. "Something like that."

"I'll be honest, I was expecting you to come out tomorrow morning," Howie tells me as we walk through the woods, the smell of decaying wood and leaves wrapping around us, rivulets of rainwater trickling along the path. We step over fallen tree trunks and hear the wind whistling through the leaves.

"Sorry for putting you out," I tell him. "I just couldn't let it go once I read the report. Once I saw the photos, I had to get started."

"I get it," Howie says with a nod, pushing aside wild blackberry vines that cover the path. "You've got to approach each case like it's your last. Otherwise you're not doing the job justice."

Whatever I thought of Howie when we met a few minutes ago has changed. He may be weathered by the worries of life, but he has a heart. He has a pulse. "Look below," he says, "this is the ravine where Kevin was found."

I give a long whistle. "Damn, that's a fall."

"I know, right? And the crazy thing is there are no tracks at all.

Whoever did this knew what they were doing because they covered it up."

"That or the rain," I say.

Howie shakes his head. "It hasn't rained in three days out here. No, nothing got washed away that night. This downpour just started, which means whoever did this knew what they were doing. Or the people that he was working with did."

"He?"

He shrugs. "Those knife wounds were pretty substantial."

I nod, computing what he's saying. "And he was alone, right? No word on his sister?"

"Nothing. If they were together, they were separated at some point over the last seven years. I wish we knew more of the story. No one has identified Kevin. No one's come forward about his death. Nothing. It's like he was never here at all."

I squat down, surveying the scene from another angle, looking out at the ravine and then back again at the lush forest behind us. These woods are filled with trees that are a thousand years old, cedars reaching up to the sky, their branches towering over us. Below, the ground is a carpet of moss and thick growth.

Underneath a neon green fern, though, I notice something. I point it out.

"What is it?" Howie asks with a frown, pulling up the broken fern frond. Nestled beneath the leaves is a small stuffed doll.

It's not that dirty, and it's not that wet. It hasn't been out here for days, that's for sure. It's a small cotton filled doll, handmade, wearing a plain white dress.

I look at Howie. "Whenever Kevin came out to these woods, he sure as hell wasn't alone. Megan was with him."

7 WILLOW GRACE

I WAKE WITH A START, spilling the ice-cold tea down my T-shirt. "Crap," I groan, setting the file folder that is lying across my lap on the coffee table and placing the now empty mug of tea beside it. The motion activator is buzzing, having gone off, tripped somehow. I immediately feel on edge, my heart pounding as I walk to the control panel, shutting it off.

Reaching for a flashlight, I unlock the door to go check it out. I'm immediately reminded that it's three in the morning, pitch dark, cold enough to send a shiver over me, and pouring rain. I jam my feet into a pair of worn boots and head outside, scanning the yard for movement. In the distance, though quite far off, I see flashlights.

I frown, wondering who would be this close to my property, and I grab a pair of binoculars. But the fact it is the dead of night keeps whoever is out there from view. They're much too far away. There's no way in hell they're the ones who tripped the sensor. They couldn't have run that fast.

I swallow, my pulse still quick. Flipping on my flashlight, I take in the area around my house, pausing on the deer that is eating salal berries that are growing in the underbrush at the edge of my porch.

Big brown doe eyes stare back at me, as if confused that I have approached her. She must be hungry to be out in the rain like this.

A moment after my light catches her, she jumps, skittering off into the orchard, away from my cabin.

I exhale, my head falling back, both feeling like a fool and vindicated. The motion detectors work. That's something. And even though it was just an animal – and not one that is any threat to me — it gave me something new to observe.

Whoever is far off in the distance, nearly over the hill, is closer than I want. Closer than I like. I don't want anyone to find me. I don't want to be known. I've never invited a single person to my cabin, and I don't intend to anytime soon.

I walk back inside, locking the door, bolting it tight. At the control panel, I flip back on the motion sensors, then I clean up the mess I made with the tea. A fresh shirt, the mug in the sink, the file folder set out to dry. In the bathroom, I splash cold water on my face, telling myself to get a grip, to go to sleep. I pop two melatonin for good measure before slipping off my boots and crawling into the warmth of my bed.

Sheets on skin. Wool blanket pulled up to my chin. Eyes closed. Breathing deeply, I let my belly rise, belly fall. As I try to fall asleep, I focus on the meditation exercises my therapist taught me all those years ago when I was learning to navigate the world for the first time in my life. *It's okay. I'm okay. Nothing will hurt me. Not today.* I repeat my mantra, hoping that if I say it enough, it might come true.

With the light of the full moon shining through my curtained window, I fall asleep, but I don't dream. The only thing I ever have are nightmares.

8 PAXTON HOLT

FINDING that stuffed doll was just what we needed to move forward. It makes me feel justified in my rash decision to come out here straightaway. If I hadn't followed my instincts and waited until morning, this toy doll would've been sopping wet, Megan's prints compromised. Now, we were able to use them.

Megan Talbot was in our system from her disappearance seven years ago and now we have a reason to believe that she was in the woods with her brother the night he died. It both complicates things and makes the case much more urgent.

A now ten-year-old girl has been missing for more than half her life. We can't wait around. We need to find her now. And we need answers for Kevin's murder and why the pair was missing in the first place.

Howie's officers and volunteers arrive on the scene as soon as the prints are run. It's the middle of the night and the rain is torrential. Time is of the essence, and I'm glad Howie was able to mobilize a team so quickly.

"How you holding up?" Howie asks me.

I nod with a grimace. "Best I can. I'm wondering the same about you."

He shrugs. "Sugar and coffee keep me going."

"I'm glad so many people came out tonight to conduct this area search."

"Can't wait on something like this," Howie says. "And Sheriff Moon will be out here shortly to meet you."

With flashlights in hand, we assess the area. It's difficult. The terrain isn't easy. Many branches have fallen on the trails. Vines and brambles block our way. The forest is fighting against us. Still, we march on, looking in pairs for any clue of a little girl.

"Megan!" we call. "Megan! Can you hear us?"

Over and over again, we repeat this question wanting a different result because maybe somehow, some way, we'll get one.

She could be sleeping and not know we are out here. She could be hiding, scared to reveal herself, not knowing if we are the good guys. Whoever took her, they're the bad ones.

I want, of course, to hear the sound of a little girl whimpering in the woods. Not because I want this child to suffer, but because I want her to finally find rest, find relief. Lost in my own search, I've moved away from Howie. "You around?" I call to him.

"Over here," Howie says, flashing his light in my direction, and I hustle over.

"Did you get something?"

"No, but, Holt, I was thinking."

"What?" I ask.

"She had to have been close by, wherever they were living," Howie says. "No one would be this stupid."

"This stupid about what?" I ask him.

"To let her out here on purpose. Whoever killed Kevin is probably shaking in their boots that this little girl has gone missing the night her brother was murdered."

"She has to be hiding," I say, agreeing with him.

He nods in agreement. "If they got separated during the altercation with his killer, that means she's somewhere near us."

"No one's reported a missing child, and no one would have a reason to keep her with them without calling the cops."

We look at one another, a fear growing between us. She could be dead, too.

Finally I speak. "Let's not assume the worst until we have to."

Howie nods in agreement. "The thing about this area is we are in the middle of nowhere. People can get a little crazy when they're left alone for too long."

"Maybe she is holed up with someone out here. Maybe she is back with her captor."

Howie shrugs. "Could be. My boss is always telling me not to jump to conclusions, but I admit it's kind of hard not to."

"Jumping to conclusions or not, this girl might have been taken for a second time."

"Hell. Who would want to do that?" Howie puts words to the obvious. But the sad truth is, not everyone is sane. And in our line of work, we mostly deal with the sociopaths of the world.

At this I steel my gaze ahead, to the woods that we have yet to search. "How the hell do I know? But I'll tell you this, I sure as hell am going to find out."

9 WILLOW GRACE

Visions of that small, frail doe with big brown eyes haunt me and keep me tossing and turning all night, memories of my past chasing me as I fight to sleep.

I wake only a few hours later – knowing I won't be finding the rest I crave. When this happens, I've learned it's best to just try to start the day. When my feet hit the cabin's wooden floorboards, there's no comfort. I shiver; the rain from the night has cast a gloom over the woods. Unlike yesterday when I was walking on campus with my face tilted toward the sun and the sky, the inlet, the salt water, and the promise of something better, something new.

Right now, everything has a layer of chill, a rigidity I don't like. I wrap a sweater tightly around me and kneel in front of the fireplace, starting a fire to warm my home. I stack logs and kindling, twisting old newspapers and striking a match.

Once lit, I walk into the kitchen, putting on a pot of coffee, rubbing my eyes. It's barely five a.m., still dark outside. I should be asleep. I don't have class today.

I'm holding the glass coffee pot in my hand, full of water, when the motion detector from outside is tripped, activating again.

I shriek, scared.

The voice I let out doesn't feel like my own. I am on edge in a way I haven't been in years, and I don't like it. My heart pounds, thinking of the flashlights I saw in the distance last night. I set the coffee pot on the counter, my hand drenched from the water that spilled out of it when I was startled. Wiping my hand dry on a kitchen towel, I walk toward the front door.

If the alert was activated, it may have been that doe again, but it may have been something else. I look at the security screen that is mounted next to the front door. The alert was from the motion sensor on the porch, not from the yard.

A deer would not come that close, not for its life. My body tenses, every muscle on edge. Quietly, I walk to a drawer in the kitchen and pull out a small pistol I keep for just this reason. A potential threat is not something I take lightly. Still, even though I've practiced using a weapon plenty of times, it feels awkward in my hands. I thought I was safe out here in my bubble, but maybe I've been wrong.

I clutch it without knowing what I exactly plan on doing. Whoever is here could be arriving for non-threatening purposes. Maybe someone got lost. But I didn't hear a car roll down the driveway. More likely it is someone who knows who I am; my past has finally caught up to me. I swallow.

Violence is not something altogether foreign to me, but I am never the one inflicting it. In my experience, it has been others – the men in power – who weaponize their strength. I don't want to feel weak, so I carefully hold the weapon in my hand.

I don't want to use it, but I will if necessary. I don't want to hurt anyone, but self-preservation is paramount. It's what I have worked my entire adult life to achieve.

It is time to be strong, resilient, brave.

My past does not define me. My past does not define me. My past does not define me.

If I say it enough, it must be true.

I tuck myself in the corner of my cabin living room, silence filling the air as I hold my breath. The clock on the wall ticks and with each passing second, it's a reminder that time is not on my side. It never was.

Unable to hold my breath any longer, it releases rapidly with a silent gasp. A knock comes from the door. I let out a soft whimper, a sound that does not feel like my own. A sound I don't even recognize, but it's as if I'm transported in time, a little girl all over again, scared for my life.

But as I listen, I take pause. The knock jars me because I was expecting something more violent than a simple thump on the front door. It takes me a moment to realize there are no gunshots. There is no kicking in the entryway or bashing a window. The violent impact I was anticipatingdoesn't arrive.

Instead, there is a gentle knock. It comes again. The knock is soft and small, tiny.

The sound is so delicate it gives me the courage to move, to tiptoe across the creaking floor and click on the monitor. On the panel, I scroll to the camera that overlooks the front porch. I don't know what I am expecting to find, but what I see takes my breath away.

It's a visitor, all right. But not someone I know.

There is a young girl on my porch. A young girl who's looking at the door with a fear I understand. It is a look of pure terror.

I keep the gun in my hand as I approach the door, doing my best to control my breathing. Remembering that whoever this is, is not the enemy. At least not yet.

My training as a psychologist has taught me to listen, to take in all the cues before I make a move. I focus on controlling my breathing as I stand on the opposite side of the door, a wooden barrier separating me from this child.

When I finally open it after a fourth knock, the girl is standing in the shadows. It's still dark out. The sun hasn't risen, but a new day has dawned. She looks like a younger version of me – lost and alone and scared.

This child is drenched from head to toe. The rain has stopped, but there is no sun out to dry her clothes. Her long blonde hair hangs to her waist, dripping droplets on the porch. Her eyes are big like that doe, warm and brown. She stares back at me, searching my blue eyes. She's in a long white cotton nightgown that looks hand made. Something you would've seen a century ago.

She's slight but looks sturdy. Her bare feet are filthy but planted firmly on the porch. The expression etched across her face is one I know all too well. It's pure, unadulterated fear, and it's carving a river through my heart.

I look beyond the child into the night. There is the faint sound of voices and barking dogs. Someone is looking for her. She doesn't want to be found.

I bring her inside, ushering her in quickly, securing the deadbolt. Then I look at her, really look at her, trying to understand where she came from and why.

"Hello," I say softly. "I'm Willow. Do you need help? Can I help you? Do you know where your family is?"

She doesn't speak. She looks at me in shock. Her eyes fill with tears, big droplets roll down her rosy cheeks.

"It's freezing, isn't it?" I say. "It's okay. Come here. Let's go by the fire."

I quickly add more logs in the fireplace, stoking the embers of the fire. The flames burst back to life as I add kindling. She's silent, holding her arms around her body, shaking.

"I'm sorry," I say gently. "I don't know what you need, but I can get you some dry clothes. Okay? One second. I'll be right back. Or you can come with me if you like."

She doesn't speak nor does she follow. I hustle to my bedroom, opening my drawer and pulling out a sweatshirt. I carry it back to her along with a blanket. "You can wear this like a dress," I say. "And you need to warm up. Wrap up in this blanket and sit in front of the fire, okay?"

She doesn't say anything, but she takes the sweatshirt and then lifts her nightgown, letting it fall to the floor with no pretense, no shame or embarrassment. She's simply getting dressed. She slides on the sweatshirt. It's huge on her, hanging to her knees, but that's the point.

"May I take this?" I ask her, reaching for her soaked nightgown.

She nods. That's something. She sits closer to the hearth, the fire emanating a warmth we both need. She wraps her arms tight around her bent legs, and she rocks without control over her body. I take the nightgown and lay it across the hearth to dry.

"It won't take long," I say. "If you want to be back in your own clothes soon, you can. Okay? Do you want a hairbrush? Do you need some hot cocoa?"

She doesn't speak.

"Do you know where you're from? Is there someone looking for you?" I ask as gently as possible, but the girl says nothing. "Did something bad happen?"

At that, she turns her head ever so slightly in my direction and gives me the tiniest of nods. She doesn't speak, but it's progress. I don't want to get this wrong. I want this girl to be safe, to be where she belongs.

"Is there someone else out there? Someone who's looking for you?"

She finally stops rocking, and for the first time, I'm not getting a sidelong glance, I'm getting a look straight into my eyes. She gives me a look that says, yes, someone is looking, yes, something bad did happen. Yes, I am scared.

The fear in my body worsens as I realize that whatever has happened to this child is no small thing. But I don't want to put her on higher alert than she already is. Her body is shaking, her eyes frozen with fear. "I think you might need some help. Can I help you?" I ask.

At this, the small girl gives a more definitive nod. She needs me.

Standing, my body trembles against my will. All I want is for this child to be safe. The past has reached out and pulled me back – I see myself in this child. When I was young. I lived in a perpetual state of fear. I press my fingertips to my palms, the pressure alleviating my flight response.

Reaching for my cell phone on the kitchen counter, I know I must call the police. My fingers press 9 1 1. But before I press call, the child speaks. Her voice cutting through the silent cabin.

"No," she says, her word clear and firm. She may be small, but her voice is strong. "Don't call the police."

Hanging up the phone, I walk toward her, feeling the urgency of this moment.

"It's okay," I say. "We don't have to call the police right now. We can wait."

The girl walks to me, collapsing into my arms, sobbing, her narrow shoulders shaking. The embrace catches me off guard, the last thing I was expecting. A hug is the one thing that usually causes me to brace myself – but with her, I don't tense. I wrap my arms around her, letting her cry.

She may be scared of the police, but clearly, she's not scared of me.

10 PAXTON HOLT

By nine a.m. the search party is exhausted. The volunteers have other commitments and are heading out, and the officers on duty are changing shifts. The rain has died down, but the sky is blanketed in gray clouds. Heaviness weighs on me, and I know I'm not alone in that. The officers from the Thurston County Police Department are all drenched from the night's storms and exhausted from hours of walking the woods in the dead of night.

Sheriff Moon arrives at the crime scene later than I expect. But I've been told he was working on a case in downtown Olympia and wasn't able to get here any earlier. Howie, as the Deputy Sheriff, oversees this murder investigation anyway, so I shouldn't be surprised that Moon isn't taking the lead.

Upon seeing him, I walk over quickly, offering my hand to introduce myself. "I'm Paxton Holt, FBI Agent."

Moon's eyes are warm, wrinkled in the corners, and his hair is gray. He takes my hand and shakes it firmly. He smiles, putting me at ease which is impressive considering it's been such a long night.

"I'm glad you're here, son," he says, patting my shoulder with his free hand. It's unexpected, the warmth he emits. Maybe Howie had just given me a different impression of the guy. But after getting to know Howie over the course of the evening, I learned he's a bit more jaded than I realized. Sounds like he's been through the ringer with his family and what the guy could really use is a vacation somewhere warm, tropical. Get the guy a cocktail and a pool floaty for a week.

Moon, though, is different. He is a grandfatherly type. He could be Santa Claus without the beard. "So I hear you did a good job finding the toy doll," he says. "A miracle there were salvageable prints on it."

I nod in agreement, appreciating his candor. "Yes," I say. "It was good that we found it when we did. The rain just didn't stop pouring all night."

Moon looks up to the sky. "It's going to return," he says. "I'm calling off the search for now."

I frown. "Really? There are still a few areas we haven't gone through."

"Sure, I know. I looked at it on the map, and we can do that later. Everyone needs rest, you included. You've been up all night. The last thing we need is an error due to someone's exhaustion."

While I'm disappointed, I can see Sheriff Moon's logic. His experience could be helpful in this case, and while I don't agree with his point of view, I understand it. We exchange contact information and agree to get in touch later in the afternoon.

"After you've gotten some rest," Moon says with a smile and a finger wag.

"All right," I say. "Will do."

I head over to Deputy Howie and tell him what Moon shared. Howie frowns, running a hand over his salt and pepper beard. "I hate stopping before we've gotten anywhere, but I suppose everyone's tired."

"Speaking of," I say. "Do you know if there is a motel close by? I don't really want to make the trek back to Seattle, especially if we're going to be picking up in a few hours."

"Of course, yeah. There is a place. Motel Evergreen. Just three miles away. It's kind of secluded. Not exactly five-star accommodations, but ..."

"That's fine," I say. "I'm not picky. I just need a few hours of shuteye."

"I could use the same," he says.

"By the way," I say to Howie, "I'm glad you're on this case."

His lips press into a firm line, and he nods slowly. "Yeah, I'm glad you are too, Paxton. I wasn't sure about you."

"Why's that?" I ask.

Howie chuckles. "I don't know. You're young, handsome, a little cocky."

"I prefer confident," I say.

"Sure," he says. "Anyway, I hope that together, we can find this girl before ..."

I push away the fear that's been lodged in my throat since I found that stuffed doll last night, knowing the end of his sentence is, *before it's too late, before the murderer strikes again, before she's gone, just like her big brother.*

"If you want," Howie says, "I can stick around. We can continue to look. I don't want you to feel like we're wrapping up too fast today."

I shake my head. "I appreciate it. I really do, but I'm going to head out. It's been a long night."

He gives me a quick wave before he looks back out at the woods once more. I watch as he draws in a deep inhale, then exhales before he walks towards his cruiser. He looks like there's a lot on his mind, but I don't know him well enough to call him back and make sure he's okay.

Even if I did know him better, I want to check things out on my own. I'm more comfortable working alone right now, that's why I dismissed his offer. I figure I'll meet back with Howie and Moon in a few hours. For now, I want to check out the area from the road.

I get in the car and begin driving toward the motel. But instead of taking the turnoff, I continue straight ahead. As I look in the distance, I notice a tendril of smoke lifting to the sky. I slow my vehicle, assessing the area. How far is that smoke from where we've been searching? Not too far at all. I turn on my blinker, flip the car around, and head down a long driveway that has no marker, no sign, no mailbox, no address listed. But someone's out there. Someone started that fire, and I need to know who.

11 BENJAMIN SHAW

When we moved here eight years ago and formed The Harmony, the intent was pure. To create a simple life for a group of people who were humbly committed to leading a life of harmony, distraction free, focused on caring for the earth and the people on it. We are committed to living a life of purpose.

We've kept our membership small. Seventy of us live here. And as I walk through the grounds now, I see the fruition of our labor: the grace and ease among the children, the women and men working as one, the fields, the homes.

We have a simple existence, hunting for animals, cultivating gardens, woodworking and operating a blacksmith shop. We forge our own way in the world we've made for ourselves. We don't abhor technology, but we know the evils of leaning upon it too heavily. I know this from my own experience, of course, but also from the stories of the other members of our community who, over time, have learned that living without excess has allowed us to become more aligned with the land. We are living a life with a singular motive to leave this world better than we found it. Also, we understand the importance of physical gratification, which is why many men are drawn to our community. Here we understand a woman's role and a man's place.

My new wife, Hannah, smiles at me, a basket in her arms as she joins me, linking her arm with mine. "Hello, Father," she says, leaning over and kissing my cheek. She's a beautiful bride, young and fertile, and the baby she carries will be a boy.

"What did you gather?" I ask, looking down at her basket.

"The last of the season's collard greens and some onions." She smiles up at me. "I'll add them to the roast chicken I'm making tonight."

"You're a good woman," I say. "Now, run along. I have work to do." And I do – last night was a disaster and once everyone learns what has happened, the community will want answers.

"Yes, Father," Hannah says, leaving me be. I watch as she joins my other two wives. Hannah is my newest bride and my greatest gift. I've watched her grow from a child. And now she is a woman. Pride fills my chest as I look over the community I've created.

There are fifteen houses in a circle all painted white, and in the center is our square. Beyond the homes are our sheds, our barns, and our workshops. I enter the center square for a meeting. We conduct most of our business outdoors when we can under a covered awning. I don't want to be boxed into a building – when I am out in the open the community can see my influence. And that is essential – especially for the children. They need to understand I am always watching.

Since it stormed all night, things are still wet and muddy this morning, but nothing's ruined by rain. Instead, it's wiped clean. It's a gift, to be sure.

"Earl," I say, addressing the young man who's been tasked with bringing back our lost sheep. They weren't always lost. When we first found them abandoned on the streets of Seattle, my right-hand man, Jordan, knew they needed to be saved. It was a gift when they joined our community. Everyone knew it and felt it. And Jordan's family took the children under their wing, just as they have with six other abandoned children. It is one way we give back to the world, take in the ones who are lost, offering them refuge and teaching the value of a life of service and penance.

At the time, Jordan and his wife were unable to conceive. It was a gift from the universe that they were brought to us when they were. Now, though, Kevin and Megan have grown. And I think Kevin's early years in the world made him hard in ways the community can't comprehend. Why fight against the bylaws of Harmony when following them will make your life so much better?

Kevin is smart, capable – if he applied himself to our teachings, he could grow to be an important member of our community with several wives and many children. He has that choice. But instead of leaning into the opportunity, he acts as though being here is a punishment.

We want harmony more than anything. Kevin, for years, has been hell-bent on discord. Megan, of course, is a child, barely ten years old, always with her hands in fists. Tough and hard. In that regard, she's like her brother. He's barely a man, and his ethics show it. Instead of putting in time and labor in the fields, he's constantly looking for reasons to argue, to fight back against our order. Questioning everything when his role is to be silent unless asked.

Earl has been close to him since they were children. Nearly the same age, the two boys spent many years as friends. But time has changed their dynamic. Earl has grown into a fine young man who is strong, resilient, and understands the virtue of togetherness.

However, right now, he has disappointed me significantly by failing the one task which I asked of him.

I pull out a chair and sit down at the table. I know eyes are watching us from all over the town square. Wives and men, children too.

"I'm sorry," Earl says. "It was an accident. I didn't mean for him... I didn't think it was..."

"What were you planning to do with that knife? Why would you have taken it at all if you weren't intending to use it?" I ask. My voice is even and firm. I am not an authoritarian. I am a father.

"I thought I could use it to threaten him, you know, scare him a bit, but..."

"And is that all you did?" I ask him. He's crying now. Shaking. It's such a contrast to his stature and his normal focus on being tough.

"No," he says, "I didn't think I was going to. It just got..." He shakes his head. His words lost.

"Spit it out," I say, my tone tight.

"I didn't mean to stab him. I just thought... I was trying to get his attention. Get him to stop. He was trying to fight me. I wasn't expecting that. You know how Kevin is. He's so weak. He's such a pansy."

"Don't speak like that of your brother," I say. And even if I agree with him on the description of Kevin, I would never say it out loud. I honor each of the members of this community equally. I fold my hands together on the table. Regardless if it was an accident, the fact that Kevin is dead has created a grave problem.

His mother, Jordan's wife, Lucinda, is distraught. She wants to know where her children are. "What do you plan on telling Lucinda?"

"I don't know," he grovels. "What do you want me to tell her? I'll tell them the truth, anything."

"You're going to tell their mother that you killed their son and her little girl is missing?"

"What do you think I should do?" Earl asks, begging for help.

"I think you should have thought this through before you killed a brother and lost a child, Earl. I thought I could count on you. We knew they were escaping, and I thought you could bring them back by reasoning with them. It was a simple job."

"But I'm only twenty," he says, defeated. "Why didn't you do it? What did you want from me?"

I won't let him know this, but of course I wanted to test him to see his strength. And now I wonder if I had gotten it all wrong.

I thought Earl Dawson was a member I could count on. Now, I'm not sure he can even be trusted. "You're going to tell their mother what you've done."

"And then what?" he asks. "Will you punish me? Am I going to be in trouble? Am I?"

"You said it was an accident, right?" I reply with a force he isn't expecting.

"It was," he said. "I didn't mean for him to fall over the ravine. I didn't even mean to stab him in the back. I thought...I don't know what I thought. I just..." Tears spill from his eyes, and I hate the weakness he is displaying.

"You thought you were helping him," I answer for him, giving him the words, a story, the new version of what transpired. I wasn't in the woods, so I will never know, but I can guess that Earl's anger took over. When he realized Kevin was stronger than he anticipated, he used force to get what he wanted, which was a mistake because now Kevin is dead, and Megan is missing, and the mess is goings to be a hell of a lot bigger to clean up than I want.

"But all of that can be healed in time as long as this stays within our family, within Harmony. Do you understand me?"

Kevin wipes his eyes, regaining his composure. "Yes, Father. Yes, Father, I do understand. And I'm sorry. I..."

"Do not apologize for anything but the accident," I say. "You go explain the situation to Jordan and Lucinda. We'll talk later."

He gets up and leaves as another man, Ezra, walks over. "Father Benjamin, there's a police cruiser pulling up at the gates. The officer is asking to see you."

I nod, thanking him for the information as I head toward the police. As I approach the cruiser, I'm not sure who I will see inside. It's always a crapshoot in this neck of the woods. We are off the grid, off the beaten path. However, occasionally we are forced to encounter the world at large.

Still, every time we have the opportunity to engage with the world, we do our best to put our truth forward, leading with love and grace. When I see who it is though, I relax. He is one of us.

"How can I help you?" I ask, knowing why he's here. "It's terrible what's happened," I say.

"You heard then about the girl that's gone missing?" he asks. "The boy who is dead."

I tense, meeting his gaze. He understands the impact more than anyone. He looks exhausted and I am not surprised – this situation is going to be a complete headache for him, all because Earl and Kevin couldn't keep their heads on straight.

"We know," I say. "And it is making a big mess over here."

"A mess within the police department too. This isn't gonna wrap up with a bow," he grunts.

"Any luck locating the girl?"

"Not yet, but we'll be picking it back up in a few hours. I wanted to know if anyone from your community wanted to come out and help. The search party will probably be meeting about two o'clock this afternoon."

"I appreciate it," I say. "I think there's a few young men I can have come out and assist. Earl Dawson will lead them."

The officer frowns, "Not sure that's the best idea, but I'll let you make that judgment call."

"Anything else?" I ask him.

He shakes his head, his eyes heavy with whatever he plans to say next. "The thing is, we've got a problem, Father Benjamin."

"What's that?" I ask. "I'm guessing it's nothing you can't fix." I look him dead in the eye, not wanting to believe he can't solve this with his assets as an insider at the PD.

But the officer doesn't agree. "Problem is the FBI is now involved."

12 WILLOW GRACE

Over the last few hours, I've learned a few things from this girl, even though she hasn't spoken a single word since she requested I not call the police. She may be small in stature, but she has grit in her eyes, determination. A strength I didn't initially notice. Her bare feet may have been caked in mud and her fingernails too, but her shoulders pull back when she looks at me, and she's not scared to meet my gaze. It's like she's searching me for an answer. There's a question on the tip of her tongue, and I want her to feel safe enough to ask it.

I start by cleaning her up. I draw a bath for her with warm water and root around the cupboard underneath my bathroom sink for some soap I can use for bubbles. Surprisingly, I find a maternal instinct kick in, remembering in my own childhood, I didn't have such luxuries as bubble baths, and I'm thinking this little girl may not have either. She looks all alone in the world.

When the water is ready, I walk out to the living room where she's still huddled by the fire, looking in the flames as if she's going to find something there too. It makes me wonder what this girl has seen, what she's scared to say.

"I think you need to get cleaned up, sweetheart," I tell her gently.

I kneel on the floor next to her. I don't want to touch her to scare her off, but I want her to know it's safe here to get cleaned up.

She looks over at me, her eyes sad, as if resigned. "Okay," she says. The two syllables are so soft they're barely audible, but she stands, and I show her the way to the bathroom.

"I'm going to leave the door open a crack. But you have plenty of privacy. Just pull the shower curtain around, okay?"

She nods, then looks around the bathroom with curiosity. Her fingertips run across the beadboard paneling and the light switch. Her fingers flip it on and off as if it's something unique.

She smiles softly for a moment, but I see it, though she quickly hides it again. I step away, standing in the hall, my back to the wall, wanting to be sure she gets in the tub. She needs to warm up, and she will feel so much better once she isn't shaking from the cold.

I hear her drop her clothes to the floor and pull back the shower curtain. I hear the plop of the water as she sinks beneath the surface. The sound settles something lodged in my throat. The girl is moving forward, slowly, sure, but she didn't stay rooted in front of the fire, frozen. This is a good sign; she is resilient.

Rubbing my temples, I wonder what I should do. If I call the police right now, I might lose her trust forever, and I have a feeling this girl needs someone in the world she can count on. I know we're strangers, but still, I want her to think I'm a safe person.

Knowing she's taking her bath, I call out to her. "I'm just going into the kitchen to make some breakfast, all right? There are towels right there next to the toilet. Do you see them?"

She doesn't answer. I'm not expecting her to. "If you need anything at all, just call for me. I'll be right here. I'm right here."

Then I leave her be. She's not so young. I'm guessing nine or ten, old enough to sit in the tub alone. And maybe she needs some time alone to collect her thoughts. Maybe once she does that, she can begin to speak.

That's something I can empathize with, not having words to explain the trauma you've endured. When I finally felt brave enough to leave, I had lost my voice entirely. I couldn't speak of what I had endured because it had been so hard for so long – my entire life. I am glad whatever this girl has been through, she has escaped it somehow; it gives me hope. She is a child with a whole life left to live.

In the kitchen, I make pancakes, mixing the batter from scratch. I slice some fruit, strawberries, a banana, and two peaches, and put them in a bowl in the center of the kitchen table. Heating a pan on the stovetop, I melt butter before I add a quarter cup of pancake mix, and then another, making small round pancakes. Since I'm not sure of her appetite, I decide to make the whole batch. After I flip them, I add them to a plate and slide them into the oven to keep them warm. I repeat the process until I make a dozen.

By the time I finish, I hear the bathroom door open with a creak. The girl shuffles toward me; she has put the sweatshirt back on. "Hey," I say. "Let me get you some socks for those toes."

I head to my room and pull out a pair of wool socks. Handing them to her, she sits in the chair at the kitchen table, pulling them on. Her blonde hair is still tangled, but her face is bright and clean. Her fingernails and toes are too. "Before we eat, how about I brush your hair real fast? Does that sound okay?"

She bites her bottom lip, looking up at me, but then she nods quickly and follows me back down the hall to the bathroom.

Once there, I drain the tub, realizing she hadn't, and pull out a comb from the drawer. I sit on the covered toilet seat while I run the comb through her long, tangled locks. Her hair is the color of honey. She smells like fresh air and dirt after the rain. She smells like a girl who is from the backwoods. But which ones? Is someone looking for her right this minute? I should have called the police immediately.

I don't want to hurt her, so I gently run the comb through her hair, taking my time. When I finish, I squeeze her shoulders. "There you go," I say. "All done."

She looks in the mirror over the bathroom sink and smiles, pleased.

"Feeling better?"

She gives me a small nod as I put the comb away and then we walk back to the kitchen. "Fruit salad and pancakes. That sound good? You can take a seat at the table right there," I tell her, and she does as I say.

I dish her up a stack of silver dollar pancakes, setting them before her with a jug of maple syrup. "Have as much as you like," I say. At that, her eyes get bigger, and she pours out the syrup decadently. That makes me smile. I want her to feel safe enough to eat that sugary sweetness without hesitation. She eats the pancakes by the forkful and digs in the fruit salad for the peach slices and the strawberries. "I'm not surprised," I tell her. "Most people don't like bananas so much, especially if there are strawberries and peaches to contend with. No problem. I'll eat the bananas," I say, using my fork to jab them out of the bowl, popping them into my mouth with a smile.

She doesn't say anything, but she also isn't crying and isn't shaking. I consider those things both a win. "Now listen," I say. "I know you told me you didn't want me to call the police earlier, but eventually I think we might need to go. We've got to find where you belong."

At that her eyes fill with tears, and she shakes her head fearfully.

"Don't worry," I say, trying to ease her fright. "I'm not going to leave your side. I'll go with you to the station, and if the police want to ask questions, I'll be right there with you."

She's trembling now, her chin quivering, and it makes me ache seeing her raw emotion. The last thing I want to do is trigger her with this plan, but it is inevitable. I can't keep her here without notifying the authorities.

"It must be scary," I tell her. "The idea of going to the police. They might ask questions you're not ready to answer. How about we practice here at home? My home. You could answer a question for me, maybe?"

She doesn't shake her head no at this, so I continue to press. "How about an easy one? You could tell me what your name is."

At that, she sets down her fork, using the cloth napkin to wipe her mouth. "My name's Megan," she says. Her voice is small like a bird, and I smile widely at her, relieved that she is trying. It is a good sign for the long road I know she has ahead.

"Well, it's so good to meet you, Megan. Like I said, I'm Willow Grace, and I live in this cabin all by myself, so it's great to have some company. I don't usually have people over for pancakes."

She doesn't respond to that. She just eyes me quizzically. For a moment I think she might say something more, but before she can, there's a knock on the door, not a soft knock like hers was.

This one is hard, fierce. Rapping quickly. I look out the window and see it's raining again. It's actually pouring. With a sigh I realize I never reactivated the motion sensors and alarm after I brought Megan inside. I was so consumed with her needs that I didn't even think about the security system being off. Now I feel like I could kick myself. I needed that warning. I needed that moment of time to prepare for a predator.

Megan must notice my fear. She looks at me, tears in her eyes. "It's okay," I say, thinking if I say it out loud, it must be true.

Megan, though, doesn't seem to believe me. She moves from the kitchen to the fireplace, returning to the position of her hands wrapped around her knees, shaking in terror.

Dammit. It's the last thing I want right now. I'm trying to move her away from that place of primal instinct into something less threatening. I stand as someone continues to bang on the door. I grab the small pistol from the drawer in the kitchen, and then I peer through the camera on the panel mounted next to the front door. I see a man in an FBI windbreaker with a badge and gun clipped to his hip.

The FBI? That's the last thing I was expecting.

I look over at Megan, wondering what in the world she is involved with. "Listen, sweetie, it's okay. It's the police, and the police are here to help, all right? The good news is we're not going to have to go to a station right away. They're here instead."

My anxiety is skyrocketing, though, because she's so nervous. Not wanting to open the door with a gun in my hand, I slip it in the back of my pants before answering. I pull open the door, and I paste a smile on my face just like I would if I was at Conifer College teaching a class.

"Hi," I say. "I'm Willow Grace. How can I help you?"

The officer looks at me in surprise. Not sure what he thinks when he looks at me. I'm a woman in her mid-30s wearing jeans and a t-shirt without a bra because I forgot to put one on. My hair is a mess in a bun on the top of my head. My bangs are disheveled, and I probably have dark circles under my eyes from not getting any sleep. I can only imagine what he sees.

Even though he is dripping wet, like the way Megan was when I met her only a few hours earlier, he doesn't look like he's been blowing in the wind. He looks sturdy, grounded, hands on his hips, eyes meeting mine. He's handsome. Hair cropped close to his head, piercing blue eyes. The color of the ocean, deep, dark, midnight blue. He has a five o'clock shadow. His hair is light. His face chiseled in a way you get when you're from somewhere like the East Coast or a prep school, where he might have rowed in college. A steady, good-looking man who looks well-adjusted and confident.

"Good to meet you, Willow," he says. "I'm Agent Paxton Holt." He offers me his hand, and I hesitate before taking it. "Look," he says, "I saw your fire."

"You're here because of a fire?"

"No," he says, shaking his head, rubbing his temples. A motion I was just doing. At a second look I realize maybe he is as exhausted as me. He's just so good looking it was easily masked, but now I see he's tired. His eyes are bloodshot, and that five o'clock shadow is probably something he usually shaves.

"I'm sorry, not an actual fire. I saw the smoke from what I'm assuming is a fireplace," he says.

"Right," I say, wanting to follow along. "Yeah, I have a wood burning fireplace inside." I pause, wanting to play this right. "Did you need something?"

"Actually, yes. I was hoping you might be able to help me. I'm here because there's been an incident in the woods not too far from where you live. About two miles away actually."

"Oh," I say, processing the word incident. Was Megan involved? "I thought I saw someone out in the woods last night around three in the morning."

"That would've been the Thurston County Sheriff Department. We had a search party out, volunteers too. There was an accident down at the ravine. A young man died there yesterday. He was discovered by a hiker, and we are trying to locate this boy's sister. We have reason to believe they were together when the incident occurred."

"Sister," I repeat, shaking my head.

"Yes," he says. "This young girl is presumably in trouble. She's been missing for quite some time."

"How long?" I ask.

"Seven years."

I gasp at that. "Seven years? How old is the child now?"

"Approximately ten. She was in a missing person's case in Seattle. It's unrelated to this specific incident as far as we know. However, we have reason to believe she is lost and alone in these woods. If there's anything you know that could help, your willingness to cooperate would be extremely helpful. There's not many houses out here, so to get a person to answer the door who might know something..." He looks me up and down. "Could be a real help."

I take in his words. He wants my cooperation. And as a federal agent, he deserves it. But I do not want to be dragged into a messy investigation. I need to keep myself out of the limelight. Still, Megan deserves an advocate. I know in my heart I can be here for her, even if it is hard.

"Do you know how this boy died?" I ask. "You say a hiker found him in a ravine? Was it an accident?"

At that the agent tenses. He runs a hand over the back of his neck as if rubbing out something that pains him. "It's unknown at this time. I was coming, not because of the boy, but because of his sister, the girl. She will have answers, and we need them to find the cause of death."

"A ten-year-old girl," I say again, lips twisting as I make a decision.

He nods. "Do you know anything? Anything at all?"

I press my lips together, and then I pull the door open wider. Looking over at the fireplace, I know Holt's eyes follow mine.

They land on Megan.

13 WILLOW GRACE

THE MOMENT HOLT lays eyes on Megan, the mood shifts. Complete relief washes over his face. I realize then he must have feared the worst, that this little girl was dead just like her brother. And even though she is shaking with fear, trembling with uncertainty, she is breathing. She is alive.

"Come in," I say, opening the door so he can enter.

He steps inside the warm cabin, stomping his boots on the mat. "Sorry about tracking in all the mud", he says. "I'm soaking wet." He bends down to remove his boots.

"It's all right," I say. "You can hang your jacket up if you'd like." I point to the hook next to the door.

He unzips it and hangs it to dry. "How long has she been here?" he asks.

"A few hours."

He frowns. "And you didn't call the police?"

I look over at Megan, thinking of her as my first priority. "Megan was scared. She just now told me her name. I didn't want to frighten her more. She didn't want me to call the police."

He eyes me wearily. "And you decided to listen to a child instead of..."

"I know how that sounds, but look at her," I say. "I was compelled to comfort her first, and I planned on taking her into the station after I got her warm and fed. We were just talking about it when you knocked on the door."

Holt looks over at Megan as if wanting her to confirm the story. She gives a brief nod, and for that I am grateful. She didn't need to do that, but I can already sense her loyalty is turning toward me. I am her safe haven in the middle of this storm. It's not a role I asked for, but I will take it if it helps get her to safety.

"When she got here, she was freezing, wet and hungry. She just took a bath and got cleaned up. I don't have any clothes for her. Hers are still damp," I say, pointing to the nightgown hanging near the fireplace. I realize then how stupid I am. I could have put it in the dryer, for goodness' sakes.

Holt seems to be taking this information in as well. "And you live here alone?" he asks.

I nod. "Yeah," I say. "This is my cabin."

"I didn't see a house number out on the road or a mailbox."

I shake my head. "No. My mail comes to the school where I work."

"Interesting," he says, looking over at Megan. "All right, so did you get enough to eat?"

She doesn't say anything. She will only make eye contact with me. "Would you like to sit down?" I ask Holt.

He says sure, but instead of sitting on the couch, he goes to Megan's side and sits down in front of the fire. She looks over at me, her eyes widening as if she's scared to be so close to a man she doesn't know.

I choose to sit opposite her. "It's all right," I say. I rest a hand on her shoulder and squeeze it. Holt eyes all of this with suspicion. "Look," I say. "She's pretty traumatized, so can you go easy on her, at least for a little while until she can--"

"Thanks for the input," he says, cutting me off. "But I know what

I'm doing.'."

I lift my eyebrows, realizing his confidence is veering towards cockiness. "Right," I say, not wanting to get in a power struggle with anyone, especially not a uniformed man like him.

"So, Megan," he says. "Do you want to tell me about where you've been all night?" She doesn't answer. "I found something of yours in the woods I think you might have left behind."

Her face scrunches up with confusion. "A doll. I found it hiding underneath a fern. I think it was playing hide and go seek."

From my professional experience as a psychologist, I know Holt's words would usually get at least a bit of a smile out of a child, but Megan is resolute. She refuses to engage with him.

"It was a doll in a pretty dress; looks like someone spent a lot of time making it. I was impressed."

I look at Holt wondering if I assessed him wrong. I thought he was cocky, but now he is charming, really trying with Megan.

"Anyway," he says, "the doll is at the sheriff's office, so I thought we could go down there together, and you could be reunited with your friend. What do you think?"

His logic is pretty sound, and I would've tried something along those lines myself. Even so, Megan doesn't budge. She doesn't give him the slightest indication that she's heard him, let alone agrees.

"So the thing is," Holt says, "I'd like to do this the easy way, which is you agree to come see your doll. We can drive there together."

"All of us?" she asks.

Holt pauses. "Well, you and me. We could get in my car and head down to the station, see your dolly, who I'm sure has a name, though I don't know it yet, and you can answer a few more questions for me and my friends. What do you think?"

Megan has tears in her eyes, and she clings to me, wrapping her arms around my torso, holding me tight. "Don't make me go!" she cries. "I don't want to go with him." Her fervor surprises me. She has been so quiet – but now the fear is back and stronger than ever.

"Hey, it's okay, Meg," I say. I pull her back, looking into her eyes, my hands on both sides of her arms. "Listen, it's going to be all right. Everyone wants the best for you."

But even as I say it, I realize how false those words are, especially to a child who's just been through so much. Everyone isn't there to keep her safe and protect her. There are so many people in this world whose mission is to hurt, to harm, to destroy, to ruin. And I'm guessing that Megan and her brother experienced quite a bit of that over the last seven years since they were abducted.

"I could come with," I say to Holt, "if that might help."

"I don't know," he says. "I've really got to bring her in, and no offense, but I don't want to change the questioning."

"I understand that," I say, not wanting to push myself in a situation I'm not wanted. Still, I sense Megan needs me.

But Megan is now crying even harder. "I won't go without Willow. I won't go without her." She holds me tight.

Finally, Holt runs his hand over his jaw. "All right, let's just go," he says. "The last thing I want is for Megan to have a panic attack." He looks over at her. "You've already been through so much."

Megan seems relieved by this, but only slightly. She wipes her eyes and pulls back from me.

"Honey," I say to Megan, "I'm going to go get changed real fast. You stay here with Agent Holt, and I'll be back in a minute. I'm just going to go to my bedroom."

I give him a quick smile and then head down the hall, passing the door I have padlocked. My jaw tenses, hating that an FBI agent is in my home.

While I don't technically have to change, I need to be alone. And while putting on a bra would probably be a good thing, the main reason I'm going to my room is so I can get rid of the gun. Sure as hell not going to a sheriff's office packing heat.

When I come back out of the bedroom wearing a sweater, socks, and shoes, I notice Holt looking at a door next to the kitchen, the door with the padlock. My jaw tightens as I watch him considering the security. He runs his hand over the padlock as if checking to see if it's locked.

"Where does this go?" he asks.

"The basement," I lie. "Old house."

"Right. I noticed you have a pretty state-of-the-art security system too," he says, pointing to the panel by the door.

"Yeah. Being out here all alone can be a little intimidating." I look over at Megan. "Hey, I was thinking, I don't think I have shoes quite your size, but I have some fuzzy boots that might work. Do you mind them being clown shoes for a little bit?" I ask her.

She shrugs, and I take that as a yes. I open the hall closet and pull out a pair of Uggs, offering them to her. She tucks her feet inside, and though I know they are a few sizes too big, she doesn't complain. I pull a winter coat from the closet. "You can put this on too. I'm not sure how warm you are or how cold."

Megan gives me the tiniest of smiles, which I'll take as encouragement. Holt, though, keeps examining the security panel.

"That's a lot of motion detectors."

"There are a lot of animals out here," I say, trying to throw him off.

"Right. Maybe I should invest in something like this. What did it set you back?"

"You don't have a security camera at your home?" I ask, evading the question. How much I spend to protect myself is none of his business, and I know he is just trying to pepper me with questions to see if there are any gaps in my story.

"I live in an apartment," Holt tells me. "Never really thought about it, but hey, now I feel pretty lame compared to you."

Not wanting him to consider my security features any more than he already has, I say, "Well, everyone has a past. I keep mine locked up tight."

"Just like that door?" he asks, pointing to the padlock.

I refuse to tense or give him any clue about who I am. "Sure," I say with a forced smile. "Just like the door."

14 PAXTON HOLT

The interview room is quiet. Deputy Sheriff Howie and I are trying all sorts of tactics to get this girl to talk. But you could hear a pin drop, and that's not a good thing.

Right now, we want the person we're interviewing to be talking, to be answering our questions, but no line of questioning seems to be working.

Megan is quiet as a mouse. She's looking at us without interest or curiosity, instead, it's terror. The way the light reflects in her eyes scares me. Not because I'm scared of her, she is a ten-year-old girl, but because I know you only have a look like that if you've seen things you wish you hadn't.

The case I just closed earlier this week feels uncomfortably familiar. Children who had been hurt by a man four times their age, a man who used and abused and took away their innocence. I don't know if Megan has been hurt the same way those children have, but they've been to hell and back all the same. I'm just trying to understand what kind of hell Megan has seen precisely. She stares at me for so long. The fear that's etched on her face causes me to wonder if this is the right way to go about getting information.

A camera is rolling, recording everything, and in many ways this is the best opportunity to get court admissible information, but at the same time, I feel like there's a block. There's something between us, a wall I can't crack.

Deputy Howie clears his throat. He still looks like hell, and he is looking at her, this little girl, with an uncomfortable gaze. He doesn't like this anymore than I do, though I suppose I'd be worried if there was anyone who did.

"I need to understand, Megan," I try again, "what exactly happened the night your brother died? Where were you coming from?"

Silence. I try another approach.

"Is there somewhere you were going? Did your brother have a plan?"

Again, nothing.

"I noticed there are no injuries on your body. No cuts or bruises, no scrapes. That makes me think wherever you've been, you haven't been hurt. Would you say that's true? Are you in any pain, Megan?"

Silence. It's deafening.

Howie clears his throat. "Maybe you'd like some water," he says to Megan.

She says nothing, but he scoots out of the metal chair all the same leaving me alone with her. "I'll be right back. Coffee?"

I nod, and he leaves quickly, as if he wants to get the hell away from the situation.

It surprises me because yesterday he seemed so sure that he wanted to get to the bottom of this. Now, he seems skittish, scared about something too. I'm glad he stepped outside because it's clear the uniformed deputy has been adding a barrier to the interview.

Alone with Megan, I continue to press her for more information. "Can you remember the person who was with you that night in the woods? The person who hurt your brother? He was stabbed. Did you know that?"

Her eyes widen. She bites her bottom lip. She doesn't speak.

"Before that night, it has been a long time since anyone has known where you or Kevin were. You were kidnapped when you were young. Do you know what that means?"

She stares at me blankly, but then she begins twisting her fingers together, cracking her knuckles. A move that I don't often see little girls make. It reminds me that there's a grit to her. Even though she's small, she's strong. "You were very young at the time of your abduction, only three years old. Do you remember this? Do you remember what happened when you and Kevin were taken?"

Beyond the silence that's palpable, there's a growing edge of frustration in my voice, and even though I try to not let it show, it's impossible.

"Megan," I try again. "I want to understand where you and your brother have been for the last seven years. That's a long time. Most of your life." She frowns but doesn't answer. Instead, she looks over to the two-way mirror. I know Willow is standing in the room on the opposite side with Sheriff Moon, but I can't imagine Megan knows that. Then again, I don't know what this girl knows, where she's been, who she's seen, what she's done. That's the problem. She is a locked box, and I don't know the combination to open the door.

I think about the lock on the door at Willow's house, and how unusual it is to have a padlock to the basement. Who keeps their pantry items so secure? It didn't make sense then, and it doesn't make sense now. Besides, the cabin didn't seem that old. It was well maintained with nice furnishings and a well-kept property.

I look over at the two-way mirror as well, wishing I could see straight through. I want to know what Willow's doing in this moment, what she's thinking, because there was an edge to her when we met. She seemed nervous too, but different from Megan. When she opened the door to the cabin revealing Megan, the little girl wasn't the only one trembling, the only one shaking in her boots. Willow was scared too, scared of something. The motion detectors she has set up all around her home are not normal security measures. You only set up a system like that if you are hiding something.

I did my best to play it off, to act like I thought it was cool how secure she was, but the woman's living in a prison of her own making. Why?

When Megan refuses to answer anything I ask, I let her know that I'm doing my best to locate her mother.

At this, she leans in close. "My mama?" I wonder what mama means to a girl like Megan. Is it the woman who gave birth to her or is it whoever's been caring for her all this time? And even though she hasn't been with her birth family, I hope she wasn't entirely neglected. She appears nourished. She is strong and healthy, but that doesn't mean she's been cared for, I suppose.

"Yes, your mother," I say. "The person who gave birth to both you and your brother, Kevin."

Megan sits back in the chair, her brows knitting together, considering what I've just said. I know that her mother was a junkie, that her father is dead and that she and her brother were abducted when her mom was drugged out of her mind. But I'm not going to say any of that to a child. I want to do my best to protect her. And considering she was missing after seeing the murder of her brother, I'm guessing no one's been properly protecting her for a hell of a long time.

15 WILLOW GRACE

WATCHING Megan through the two-way mirror in the interrogation room is painful. That vision I had of her, of being a frightened doe, comes back to me now. Nothing's changed in her eyes since I've met her. She looks just as scared now as she did then.

When I see Deputy Sheriff Howie leave the room, I think she might relax a bit and begin to open up. She spent a bit more time with Agent Holt, and there might be room for her to feel safe enough with him to open up. In the car he put on popular music he thought she might like. He bought her a donut and a hot chocolate at a coffee shop before we got to the station.

As I noticed these things he did for her, it cemented in my mind that he is good at his job. He's trying to win her over, warm her up to him, but she is a hard sell.

Now they're alone in the room together, and while I can hear his line of questioning, she's not taking any of the bait. Whatever happened the night her brother died, she's not saying a word.

I know he's frustrated. The way the muscles in his jaw tense, the way his eyes narrow ever so slightly, the way he sits back in his chair, acting like he's completely nonplussed. But he is. I know this because I am a psychologist. I went to school to study people. Now I teach that to the students at Conifer college. Our body language reveals so much, sometimes more than we want.

A uniformed man enters the room. He introduces himself as Sheriff Moon. I stand, still watching the interrogation, but I shake his hand and tell him my name. I don't want to be difficult, especially not to the Sheriff.

Moon clears his throat. "So, it seems pretty lucky."

"What's that?" I ask, not tracking.

"That Megan found your cabin when she did."

"Lucky?" I ask with a frown, turning to face the man I've just met.

He's a grandfatherly type, with a non-threatening demeanor. But just like Howie, it's hard for me to trust him. It's hard for me to trust *any* man in authority. It's probably why I've never had a real relationship. They don't come easy to people who have walls around their heart and security systems around their home. To say I don't let people in easily is an understatement, which is why Megan capturing my heart so damn fast is an anomaly.

One that worries me slightly. Why is she so dear to me after just a few hours? Is it because she's a child alone in the world having just suffered a trauma? Or is it something else? Is there another reason I feel a connection toward her?

I can't give in to this line of thinking too far though, because Moon is asking the questions. "So what do you do out there in the woods? I heard you have a pretty fancy security system."

"Holt tell you that?" I ask, slightly surprised that he'd confide anything about me to someone else. He doesn't seem the sort, and he's an FBI agent, not a local cop.

"He mentioned it," he says. "So you live out there, work out there?"

"I live there," I say. "I have for about six years, ever since I got a job as a professor at Conifer College."

"And what do you teach out there?" he asks.

"Psychology," I say, keeping my answer simple and to the point.

I'm not going to give him any more information about me than necessary. Telling him I study cult behavior and conditioning and that I give lectures on quite specific topics about mind control isn't something I want the local jurisdiction to know. It might put a red flag on me that I don't need.

Right now all I want is to be out of the limelight. I want to keep a low profile. Being here at all contradicts my life plan.

"Interesting. A professor of psychology. Pretty fancy. You've done well for yourself then, huh?"

"Fairly well," I say.

"Well, I would be remiss if I didn't say I googled you after we brought you in."

"You googled me?" I ask, crossing my arms.

I tuck a loose strand of hair behind my ear, looking back to the mirror, watching as Howie brings in coffee and cookies. He hands a coffee to Holt and offers cookies to Megan. They're trying a different tactic. Hoping a cookie will win Megan over, but after the donut trick didn't work this morning, I'm not quite sure sugar is the way to this girl's heart.

"So what did you find when you googled me?" I ask, curious about this man's motives. Why would he concern himself with me at all?

"You wrote some books," he says.

"Yeah," I say. "I did."

"Interesting ones at that. What got you into that topic? Conditioning and behavior modification, pretty bleak subject matters if you ask me"

I didn't ask you, is what I'm thinking, but I refuse to prove myself to this man. "I studied it in college. It was part of a research project and became really interesting to me."

"Fascinating," he says, his voice flat.

"Is it?" I ask.

"Relatively," he says. "My wife, she's always watching documentaries about cults. Maybe she's read some of your books."

"Maybe," I say, not turning back to him, watching the interrogation room instead. Megan didn't reach for a cookie. She is staring at her hands, disengaged.

"Yeah, recently my wife was watching that one about that sex cult up in Buffalo. Pretty wild, right?"

"Yeah," I say, knowing which one he's referring to.

"God, if my wife came home with a brand on her pelvic bone, I think I might have a fit."

"A fit, huh?" I ask, curious. "And what would that look like?"

At that question he chuckles. "Good one," he says. "So you've been living out in that cabin for about six years?"

"Yeah. Give or take."

"It's a nice piece of property, huh?"

"Let me guess you google mapped it too?"

"Not exactly. I've never been out that way. I didn't even think there was a cabin out there."

"Yeah. I like the wilderness. In fact, I teach most of my lectures outside. There's something about being in wide open spaces that calms me. What about you? Do you do any hiking in the area?" I ask, desperate for deflection.

"A bit, but you know Howie, the deputy, he does a lot of hiking."

"Really?" I ask. I know my voice reveals my surprise. He's not exactly the most fit guy I've ever met. He looks like he's been to hell and back, but maybe he is making an effort to turn his life around.

"Yeah. He's always going off in the woods. Maybe he has a mushroom farm out there or something."

"You think he might?" I ask teasingly.

Moon shrugs. "You never know, right? These woods are wild."

"I'm not from Thurston County. I moved here for the job."

"And what do you think?"

"Well, the college is full of really creative students."

He chuckles again. "That's one way to put it."

"And what's another?" I ask.

"A lot of fringe folks, right? People looking for an alternative lifestyle."

"Sure," I say. "I've picked up on that a bit."

"A bit? Their school mascot is a clam."

"And that is problematic because?"

He gives me a grin. "Eh, what do I know? Thought it was a euphemism."

"A euphemism for what exactly?" I ask stone faced.

He looks at me then and winks. "Oh, you're something else, aren't you, Willow Grace?"

"Something else? Sure," I say, looking away as I roll my eyes, but preferring to be called *something else* than to pretty much any other way he could describe me.

"It's interesting you chose to move out there all by yourself though. Most women might be too scared to live in the wilderness without--"

I cut him off. "What, a man? Sorry. I think maybe we're different generations because I don't need a man to keep me safe."

My tone has changed, but I don't care. Let him be pissed or confused. The last thing I want is for him to think I'm weak. I've worked way too hard to break out of that stereotype.

Moon must feel the shift in my tone as well, and it's hard for me not to become defensive. "Sorry," he says. "Not my place."

I shrug, doing my best to inhale and exhale without making a scene.

"The thing is, it's a little strange, right?" he says.

"What is a little strange?"

"That this girl came to you, feels connected to you, won't talk to anyone else but you. You don't think that's odd?"

I swallow. "What are you trying to say? You think I knew Megan before today?"

Moon gives me a sly smile. "I follow the evidence wherever it leads me."

Saying no more he excuses himself, leaving me alone facing the two-way mirror, wondering who he thinks I am.

Knowing that if he really knew, my entire life as I know it would be over.

16 PAXTON HOLT

HALF AN HOUR LATER, I've gotten no further with Megan. Howie came with a cookie and left again shortly after. I could tell he's frustrated, and he's not alone in that. I was really hoping Megan would reveal something, anything that could help us, but she's been silent the entire time we've been talking.

Alone with her once more, I ask again, "Megan, I know you've had a hard day. Maybe a hard time for a long while, but what I really would love to know is if you know what happened to your brother. Everyone is working hard to figure out what happened that night. Answers will help make sure no one else is hurt. Could you at least tell me if you know what happened to him?"

At that, Megan seems to have heard me. Maybe it's my plea to protect others that causes her to lift her chin up and down ever so slightly. It's an imperceptible nod, but it's a nod nonetheless, and I got it on camera.

I don't think this girl is a liar. She holds her cards way too close to make up a story. "Thanks," I say. "Thanks for that. I know it can be really hard at times to speak the truth, to tell our side of the story, but it's really important that we use our voice when we can. There's a lot of power in it, you know."

She swallows and looks down at her hands in her lap, not saying anymore.

"Do you want to tell me about what happened to your brother?"

She bites her bottom lip, shaking her head no.

Dammit. One step forward, two steps back.

"So," I say, "you've had a donut and hot cocoa, but I'm thinking maybe you need something more substantial. Can I grab you a sandwich? Ham and cheese, peanut butter and jelly?"

She shrugs, not a word.

"All right. How about you shake your head no or nod your head yes at the one you want. All right? Peanut butter and jelly."

The smile on her face is so slight, but it's there. She shakes her head no.

"Okay and how about ham and cheese?"

She nods. I grin, relieved to make any sort of progress. "All right, I'll be right back. Hold tight."

When I step out of the interrogation room, there's a sense of relief. I'm getting somewhere, even if it's slow. She likes ham and cheese more than she likes peanut butter and jelly. That's something. And more than that, I know she was there when her brother died. She knows what happened.

Now it's about getting her to feel safe enough to open up about it.

In the hallway I'm surprised to see Sheriff Moon waiting for me. There's a look of agitation on his face that I didn't see when we first met. Before there was warmth in his eyes. Now there's a grim layer I don't quite understand. Maybe it's because I'm here in his jurisdiction, and if so, I need to be clear that I don't want to cause any problems. The last thing I need is to muck up an investigation with a turf war.

"Did you need something?" I ask him.

"Yeah," Moon says. "I do."

"Sorry that it's taking a while, but Megan is clearly still in shock. She's holding back, but I think she's going to start opening up a little bit more. I was going to go grab her a sandwich now and--"

"Look, about that. I don't think you have all the facts regarding this investigation."

"What do you mean?" I ask. "I'm literally gathering the facts as we speak."

"To some degree," Moon says. "The thing is, we've already found our suspect."

I pull back, surprised. The hallway is empty except for the two of us, and the fluorescent lighting is doing nothing but casting an eerie look on the scene. "What do you mean a suspect?"

"Well, you should know. You're the one who brought her in."

The allegation baffles me. "What are you talking about? Megan killed her brother?"

"No," Moon says, shaking his head as if talking to a fool. "Willow Grace."

"I don't think that's possible. She's-"

"No listen," he says. "Let me lay it out for you. Willow moved here shortly after the disappearance of Megan and her brother."

"What, you think she kidnapped them?" I ask. "You think she's the one who..."

"You have a reason to think she didn't?"

I pause, considering his words. What do I know about Willow? She's a woman in the woods in a small cabin with a high-tech security system that is way too state-of-the-art, considering the forest in which she lives. She is living alone, allegedly, and has a padlock door to the basement.

I tense. "What are you really trying to say?"

Moon puffs out his chest. "Look, she moved here shortly after they disappeared, right?"

"Sure, but that's not enough to make the leap that she's the abductor."

"Obviously," Moon says, "but did you happen to ask Willow about her line of work?"

I nod. "Sure. When we were driving over here from the cabin, I asked her what she did for a job. She said she's a professor of psychology over at Conifer College. Pretty impressive to be honest."

"Right," Moon says, lifting a hand. "But did you ask her what her area of expertise is?"

I hate not having an answer, especially for a man of authority like Moon. "No, I didn't ask what her expertise is. We weren't really getting into anything too deep considering we had a ten-year-old victim in the backseat."

"Sure," Moon says, with a hint of condensation. "The thing is, she specializes in cult psychology."

"Why is that relevant?"

"Because she knows how to manipulate, how mind control works. She has the skills to keep people hostage for long lengths of time."

This information surprises me. In my line of work, law enforcement, coincidence is a rarity, but it makes me wonder about Moon's rationale. Does he really think she was holding these kids captive? Brainwashing them? Manipulating them in some way?

If she's a professor, an expert in this area, would she be more prone to do that than anybody else? Maybe I have a blind spot when it comes to Willow, but I just didn't take her as an abductor.

"Look," Moon continues. "While you were with the child, I took the liberty of requesting a search warrant for the cabin. We should have our answer as to whether the good professor is involved or not soon enough."

Moon gives me a snide look, which really pisses me off. "Not sure how you fellows in the bureau do things, but around here, we like to let the evidence speak. You're free to continue the interview with the girl while we work this other angle."

"Are you kidding me?" I scoff. "You're going to go search her house, and you don't think I should be on the scene? I'm the FBI agent assigned to the case. Or maybe you forgot that."

Moon runs a hand over his jaw. "Yeah, I didn't forget. The thing is, Holt, you aren't assigned to the case, not yet. You are here for your information on the victim. And turns out, you don't have much, do you? You must feel like shit for failing these kids seven years ago, so maybe your viewpoint is skewed because of your own personal shortcomings in the first attempt to locate them." He shrugs. "And now one's dead, and the other is catatonic. Maybe you're looking past the answer that's staring you right in the face."

I swallow, but it's not embarrassment running through me, it's anger. How dare this man accuse me of not doing my job properly? He has no clue what I did or did not do to try to bring those kids home. I worked day and night for months desperate to find them, but now he's pinning this on Willow Grace? A woman who's what, a thirty-five-year-old professor? It's not possible, is it?

What else do I know about her? I rack my brain for clues, for parts of the story she might have revealed when I was at her cabin or in the car with her.

The only thing I remember her mentioning is the fact she lived alone. Her offhand comment that even if she did have a partner, she wouldn't have had children. She wasn't able to. Those words are more condemning than anything else. But why speak them so flippantly if they are vital to your alibi?

If she wanted a family, a child, what would've stopped her from taking a ten-year-old boy and a three-year-old girl? What if seven years ago she saw those kids on the street and thought this was her chance?

Still, she's a professor. She has so much on the line.

But maybe she's the perfect person to do such a thing. Keep the kids hidden away in the woods where no one knew they were around or existed and lock them up while she goes to work. I run my fingers over my temples.

"Damn," I say to Moon. "You got the warrant?"

Moon nods, and I know he feels vindicated in his decision to move forward with it. "And I got a deputy keeping a close eye on Willow until we return from the search."

"Good," I say. "In that case, I suppose we ought to go back to the woods."

17 DEPUTY HOWIE

I'M LEAVING the cafeteria when I run into Agent Holt. His face is etched with worry.

"What's up?" I ask.

"I'm getting some food for the kid."

"That all? Because usually the idea of food makes people happier, not grumpier."

"I look grumpy?" Holt shrugs. "Well hell, I suppose I am. Just talked to Moon."

"Yeah. What'd he say?"

"He's headed over to search Willow Grace's place."

My posture stiffens. "What?"

Holt gives a bark of laughter. "You didn't know? Damn, this department is interesting."

"I hadn't heard." I pull out my phone. A few missed calls and a voicemail from Moon. "Well shit," I say. "What's going on over there?"

He gives me the rundown. Apparently Willow Grace is a suspect. More than a suspect. They think she's the one who kidnapped the kids seven years ago. I give a low whistle as Holt lays it out for me.

"What do you think?" I ask him.

"I think it's pretty messy, but I suppose the search warrant of the cabin will give some answers soon enough."

"Are you headed over there now?" I ask.

Holt shakes his head. "Not yet. I promised the kid ham and cheese, so I'm getting her ham and cheese."

I smile. I'll give the agent credit. He's doing his job right. Megan should be the priority now, and I appreciate the fact he has a soft spot for a kid. Not everyone who works for the government is like that. When I first met him, I thought he was all good looks and confidence, but I'm realizing there might be a little more. He's a bit of a softie, which makes me think he's been through some hell himself.

"All right," I say. "I guess I'm headed over there now. I'll see you later?"

He nods before walking toward the cafeteria; he has a sandwich to buy.

When I pull up to Willow Grace's cabin 20 minutes later, Moon meets me on the front porch.

"I ran into Holt," I tell him. "He filled me in a bit on why you think Willow Grace has anything to do with this murder."

"Holt spoke with you? " Moon asks, shaking his head. "That guy's a real piece of work, don't you think?"

"What do you mean?" I ask. "Personally, I think he seems pretty solid. Pretty nice."

"What nice guy is an FBI agent?" Moon asks, and it's a fair enough question.

Moon steps aside, letting me know he's going to walk the perimeter of the cabin while we conduct our search. Cruz arrives with a few other officers. We enter the cabin tentatively. I've never been here before, but I can immediately tell that while minimalist, the home is well maintained. The place is small but clean. It's not that old. Probably less than fifteen years. Whoever owned it before Willow Grace insulated the place well and put in a nice wood-burning fireplace and hearth. The kitchen has newer appliances, not more than ten years old.

We enter the primary bedroom. There's a queen size bed, a dresser, and an end table with a lamp. It's all very clean, very tidy, very minimally decorated. Willow Grace is simple. That much is clear. In her closet there are sweaters, jeans, and boots. Not exactly the clothing I would expect a professor to wear, but Conifer College is a little less traditional, so I suppose she can wear whatever she wants when she's teaching.

When I enter the second bedroom, I see another queen size bed, also neatly made up, and a dresser. Inside the drawers, I find clothing that belonged to a child. I frown. The dresser drawers are full of items for a girl, dresses and nightgowns. Another drawer holds men's clothing, size small, jeans and shirts. In the closet, there's a pair of work boots along with a pair of little girl's shoes, leather with laces.

"What the hell?" I ask, looking around.

Maybe I'm an idiot, but I really didn't think the woman they brought in was capable of such a thing. She seemed so unassuming, so regular. A little skittish, sure, but she was polite in the brief moments I met her while I was getting a refill of coffee in the cafeteria. But a kidnapper? I never would have pegged her for that.

"There's a lot here," Cruz says. "All these clothes, we're going to have to get them tagged. Make sure they actually belong to the Talbot kids. This whole thing might be a bit more open and shut than we thought. Could be that the kids have been here all along, ever since they were kidnapped?" Cruz says, shaking her head.

"Wouldn't have guessed it," I say. "Hidden in plain sight."

When I pull open the top drawer of the dresser I find a gun, a small hand-held pistol and behind it there's a knife. I give a low whistle, honestly stunned.

When Holt stopped me in the hall at the station telling me what Moon was planning, I didn't think he'd actually have real evidence to charge this woman with something so heinous. But now there is a sour taste in my mouth. Maybe there is a motive I just haven't yet uncovered.

Why would she have killed Kevin? I can't help but wonder.

Moon enters the room as Cruz and another officer are photographing, tagging and collecting the evidence. "What did you find?" Moon asks.

I run a hand over my beard as I begin to show him the findings. "I think your instincts were right," I begrudgingly admit.

It's not that I don't want Moon to be correct, but it does kind of kill me. He's never given me much of a chance to prove myself and now the fact that I doubted him when he made this call makes me wonder if my instincts are wrong about everything. They were wrong about him. Maybe they're wrong about Willow. Maybe they're even wrong about Agent Holt. God knows I fucked things up with my son, with my ex-wife, with everyone in my life to be honest. The weight of that begins to gnaw at me as I stand there.

While Moon surveys what I found, the knife and the gun and all the clothing, he shakes his head. "What kind of sick fuck does this?" he asks.

"I don't know," Cruz says, "but did you see the padlocked door?"

Moon nods, but I frown. "Which door has a padlock?" I ask.

Cruz walks me through the house to a door on the opposite side of the kitchen. "Anyone find a key?" I ask the room, but they all shake their heads.

One of the officers grabs bolt cutters from the trunk of his car. Clamping hard against the metal, he cuts it open, the lock dropping to the floor, He swings open the bolt. Inside is a small room, six feet by six feet, with papers, images, and maps tacked to all surfaces of the walls.

"Well, this is unexpected," Cruz says. "Look at all this shit."

Moon clears his throat. "Funny. Down at the station, I was joking with her about how my wife likes to watch all those cult documentaries on TV. She didn't even give me any indication of how obsessed she is. Look at this."

There's cult memorabilia collected over years taped to walls, files, stacks of books, newspaper articles and clippings. There's a desk with a lamp, and I flip it on. It illuminates cases in manila folders stacked one on top of the other. Each one labeled with the name of another high-profile cult that was taken down in the United States of America over the last fifteen years. But some of the things are more shocking, more unexpected.

"Do you guys know about this one?" I ask, "The Harmony."

As I flip through the file, my eyebrows raise. I show the photographs to Cruz. Moon stands beside her nodding in surprise. "So she has some personal experience, huh? Interesting. No wonder she went into cult psychology. She'd been indoctrinated her whole life."

The photographs are pictures of Willow in simple clothing with a group of people dressed the same. Women in long white dresses with hair in braids, boys in black trousers and button-down shirts.

Cruz flips through the pictures. "This cult is still alive and well."

"What do you mean?" I ask.

"Well, people knew about its existence. It's on the outskirts of Seattle. They're called the Harmony. Anyway, there's never been enough evidence to actually take them down."

"How do you know about that?" I ask her.

She shrugs. "I don't know. I'm a millennial. We're all into that kind of shit."

I chuckle. "All right. When you say *that kind of shit*, you mean dangerous cults?"

"Exactly," she says. "Just like Moon's wife who watches the documentaries. It's pretty popular. There's a whole TikTok thing about it. I'm always watching videos about the new group down in Astoria, Oregon, or a group in Nicaragua. You know what I mean."

I shake my head. "I actually have no idea what you're talking about."

She grins. "Oh man. Howie, you're getting so old. You need to lighten up. Get with the program. Don't you have a son, Joey? Doesn't he keep you young? He should. What is he in, middle school?"

I nod. "Yeah, but we don't usually talk about random cults at the dinner table."

"Maybe you should. Might bring him out of his shell."

"I don't think the kid's in a shell. He has anger issues."

Moon chuckles. "Just like his dad."

"Hey," I say, but I can't help but smile.

This is the friendliest conversation I've ever had with my coworkers, and the fact it's in a disturbing room filled with cultish artifacts is messed up; add to that the fact it belongs to a child kidnapper? It all feels off.

"So we think Willow grew up in a cult?" Cruz asks.

Moon shrugs, lifting a nonfiction title from the pile. The author's name on the book is Willow Grace.

"Maybe she's starting some weird new cult of her own," I suggest. "Plotting things out, planning. Why else would she have all this memorabilia?"

"You think she's wanting to be a cult leader?" Cruz asks, slightly mystified.

I shrug, picking up the book and thumbing through it. When I get to the end, I look at the back jacket and see Willow's face in the author's photo. Maybe Moon isn't wrong with his theory about her.

Who becomes so obsessive about a topic like this unless they want to do something about it?

18 WILLOW GRACE

No one informed me about where Sheriff Moon and Deputy Sheriff Howie went, but they've been gone for forty-five minutes. In that time, I've watched Agent Holt bring Megan a ham and cheese sandwich, which she devoured. Chewing fast, as if she couldn't get it down quick enough. He gave her a carton of chocolate milk, which she drank with a smile, wiping her mouth with the back of her hand when she finished it. The scene relaxed me, mostly because I'm glad the little girl is getting what she wants, maybe for the first time in her life.

It's hard to know what brought her to this interrogation room. I don't know the facts or the whole story. I know she watched her brother's murder. I know she has been separated from her mother for many years. I know she is scared. These facts would make a grown-up crumble, so the fact she isn't gives me hope for her healing. She is a resilient girl and can go on to do big, beautiful things if given the chance.

Megan has been through hell, and she deserves more. But as I watch Holt, it is clear he is struggling to get anything out of her. He's resorted to using paper and crayons, hoping to elicit some form of communication with Megan. I watch as he pulls out a box of Crayons and a notebook of blank paper.

Through the two-way mirror I can hear him ask, "Is there something you'd like to draw about that night? Maybe instead of using words, you could color in a memory."

She picks up a red crayon, bringing it close to her face, studying it, reading the label. I wonder what she's thinking. I also wonder what this crayon color is called. Fire, blood, love? I haven't the faintest clue, but she holds it tight between her fingers, as if making a choice.

When she begins to draw, it's not a picture of the forest, of big pine trees, or a trail. There's no deer being depicted. No little girl and no little boy. Instead, she draws three arches, one after the other, similar to that of a rainbow. But instead of clouds at the base of each arch, she draws a straight line at an angle. I focus, not knowing what this image means to her but wanting to know very badly.

Holt asks her if she'd like another crayon from the box. She shakes her head no. "Are you sure?" he asks. "You could fill it in. Maybe that could help you tell me a story. I'd really love to hear anything you have to say."

Megan simply pushes the paper away from her, setting the crayon down with the others. She crosses her arms, making it clear she is finished with whatever game he wanted to play; Holt and Megan have reached a stalemate.

"I'm going to go to the restroom," he says. "Maybe you need to stretch your legs a bit?"

Another officer, a young woman who introduces herself as Chelsea, offers to take her outside for some fresh air. I'm glad they made that decision. This girl has been cooped up here for nearly two hours. I am exhausted standing here watching. I can't imagine how she feels.

As I'm waiting for them to get done with their break, I am surprised to see Holt enter the observation room. Another deputy accompanies him, one I've never met before.

"Hey," I say to Holt. "I noticed that drawing. What do you think it means? Have you seen that symbol before in the county?"

"Remember, I'm not from here," he says. "I'm from Seattle."

I nod. "Right, I forgot."

"But maybe I should ask you," he says. "You're from the area, right? Do you know what those three arches mean?"

I frown, shaking my head, though a part of me thinks I have seen it somewhere. But where?

The officer standing with us says he doesn't think he's seen it before either. But then he hems for a moment. "You know, it might have been carved in a tree once when I was on a hike," he adds.

I lift my eyebrows in annoyance. "Huh. Okay, well, you should write that down," I say to no one in particular, feeling like they're not taking this seriously.

Symbols like that usually mean something, and it's not something we should let go of before we explore it more.

"I'm not getting very far with her," Holt says. "She's so closed off."

"Well, that's part of the effect of long-term trauma. Whatever Megan has gone through has been significant. A form of PTSD would be the most obvious, but it could be an underlying fear of being caught by the people who have been controlling her for so long."

"People?" Holt asks. "You think multiple people have been holding her hostage?" He gives me a hard look, and I feel confused. What does he know that I don't?

"It's just an idea," I say. "Brainwashing is real, and if she thinks the place she comes from was a safe haven, then she could be resenting us right now. Maybe that's why she didn't want me to call the cops."

Another officer enters; his badge reads Thomas. "Willow Grace? I need you to accompany me to an interview room."

"Me?" I shake my head, confused.

"Yeah you." His tone is abrasive, and I look at Holt. He shrugs but doesn't intervene. Maybe he does know something I don't.

"What for?" I ask. "I told you everything I know about Megan.

She'd only been at my house a short while before Agent Holt arrived."

"I understand that's what you've been saying, but you need to come with me."

Holt doesn't interrupt or make the man stop. Instead, he nods and steps back as if he's in on this too. The look in his eyes is that of determination, as if leading me out of this room into an interrogation room isn't something he wants to be doing. It adds a layer of confusion to whatever is going on.

I want to be of help to Megan, but I'm not sure how interrogating me any further is going to do that. What would actually help Megan is letting me be alone with her to get a chance to talk to her and connect with her. With my psychological background I know I can get her to open up, but I don't feel like that option is on the table right now.

As I'm led out of the room and down the hall, I pass the room where Megan has been sitting. It's empty now, and an icy chill washes over me. A feeling that something isn't right. Something is going on – and I am getting wrapped into it. The deputy moves me along, and as I'm brought into another interview room, all I can wonder is if Holt is watching me right now. Is he taking this in from a two-way mirror? Listening closely for whatever I may or may not say?

I swallow, feeling terrified for the first time all day. Yes, I wasn't happy when the motion detectors were activated. I was scared when I reached for my pistol and crept to the door of my cabin. I was anxious when Holt looked over at Megan, taking in the scene, but this is different. This is a foreboding because I'm not in control. I don't have a weapon in my hand. This isn't my house, my home. No. This is the sheriff's department, and these men are telling me what I need to do and where I need to go.

It's a feeling that's all too familiar. My past is catching up with me.

Thomas tells me that the sheriff will be along shortly to speak with me. "Sheriff Moon?" I ask, shaking my head. "I didn't think he was the lead on the case. What about Deputy Howie?"

Thomas looks at me, his mouth set in a firm line. "I don't think you should be the one asking the questions right now. When you're on that side of the table, we're in charge."

19 PAXTON HOLT

The only plausible reason Deputy Thomas put Willow into an interrogation room is that they found something at her cabin. That idea feels like a gut punch. Am I really that off about peoples' character? Am I really that easily swayed by someone who has a compelling story? She seemed more scared than strong when I met her at her cabin. Sure, she had the padlocked room and the security system. But my first instinct was to think there are other reasons for that. Maybe she feels vulnerable. Maybe she feels afraid. Most people don't build such a defense unless they're trying to protect themselves.

Of course, my boss, Tamara Rodriguez, might challenge my thinking. She would tell me the alternative to that is she has something to hide.

I swallow. Megan did seem strangely comfortable with her. I remember the way she wrapped her arms around Willow's waist begging to stay together. She didn't want to be separated from Willow. Would a girl be that attached to someone she just met? It's hard to know, but I suppose the interrogation will bring out the truth soon enough. Coupling that with whatever was found at the cabin, I shouldn't have to wait long for answers.

When Sheriff Moon approaches me in the cafeteria where I'm taking my break, I'm surprised to see him here. I thought the search of the cabin would have taken longer than a few hours.

Megan is with a social worker having been questioned enough for one morning, and I'm carb loading. Eating my feelings while attempting to connect dots.

"You might regret that macaroni and cheese," Sheriff Moon says with a wry smile.

"Really?" I ask, taking another bite.

He nods, knowingly. "A safer bet is the tuna salad."

I chuckle. "I honestly don't think I've ever heard that statement in my life."

He shrugs. "Hey, son, can I talk to you for a minute?"

"Sure," I say. Moon sits opposite me. "First off, I wanted to tell you," I say, "that I was in contact with people at my office, and I have the Seattle Police Department trying to locate Megan's mother. She needs to know her children have been found, even if one of them is dead."

Moon nods slowly. "Good. Good."

I continue speaking. "If you'd like, I could talk to Willow and get her statement. I know you had her brought into an interrogation room, and if it could help you out, I'm available. I know you have a lot going on. A lot of moving pieces here."

"No, I don't need your help with that."

"Okay," I say. It strikes me as odd. "So who is conducting the interview?" I ask.

"I am," he says.

I frown. I didn't think a sheriff normally conducted interviews in big cases like this. "I like to step in, take care of my own." The cocky snear he has on his face when he says this unnerves me, but maybe it's my own insecurities talking. I haven't gotten far on the case. Maybe he has.

"Well, Holt, I want to let you know," Moon says. "It was a great help in finding Megan when you did." His comment confuses me.

Moon's thanking me now? "I mean it," he says. "First you found the toy doll and then you found the girl at that cabin. Hell, she could still be there for all we know if it hadn't been for your instincts and knocking on that door."

"Well, thanks," I say. "I appreciate it."

I continue eating my macaroni and cheese, and Moon asks me, "Will you meet me in my office when you're done? I have some things I'd like you to see."

"Sure," I say. "I'll just be a few more minutes."

He nods, patting the table twice before walking out of the cafeteria. I pull out my phone, texting my friend at the Seattle PD. "Any update on the Talbots' mother?"

A moment later, I get a reply. "Not yet. Working on it."

I scroll through my phone for a minute or two, wanting to distract myself from the unsettled feeling that's growing in my stomach.

Willow may have kidnapped Megan. Moon is thanking me. Howie senses a bunch of red flags.

I'm not sure what to even believe right now, what to think, but I do know Moon was right in warning me against this macaroni. It tastes like plastic. I shove my tray away and walk out of the cafeteria. My hunger is gone, replaced with a different sort of need. I want to know what Moon has to show me.

I knock on his door, and he lets me in. Deputy Howie's there already, along with several other deputies, including Cruz and Thomas, officers I've already met. They're carrying boxes into the room, and I frown, curious about what they found.

"Well," Sheriff Moon begins. "Good news is while you were conducting the interview with Megan, I executed a search of Willow's cabin."

I look over at Howie. He nods. Maybe I wasn't supposed to tell him that information, but I did. Moon doesn't need to know that though.

"Okay. You got a search warrant that fast?"

"Yes, and honestly, we probably could have gotten consent from her. She's been cooperative so far with the investigation, but we needed to move fast."

"All right. Did you find anything relevant to the case?"

"That's an understatement," Moon says. "We found plenty, and because of that, we are going to handle things on our own from here on out. In Thurston County, we do things a little different than you do over at the agency."

I don't want to get in a pissing contest over territory, but this man is mucking everything up. "You're saying you actually think Willow was involved? Truly? Because this morning when I was there, I got a different read on the situation. If you had seen Megan in that house, she was shaking. She was scared. That was before I even entered."

"Was that how it really went though?" Moon asks. "Did you see Megan shaking before you arrived or are you just assuming she was scared? Maybe she was shaking because of *you*. An officer in Willow's home. Maybe she's been conditioned to think you are the enemy."

I grimace, running a hand over my jaw, not liking the way the story keeps bending in my mind. But the more information I have, the more I must consider what is fact and what is hypothesis.

Moon clears his throat. "Look, we found plenty of evidence." He opens one of the boxes and pulls out a bag. Dried blood on the blade of a knife.

My jaw tenses. "Where did you get that?"

"In a drawer at Willow Grace's home. Odd discovery, right, if she is innocent?"

"Sure," I say. "It is. But-"

"Is there a but?" he cuts in.

I take the evidence bag from his hand looking at the knife more closely. On the handle, I see a symbol etched and carved into the ivory bone of the blade's handle. It's a symbol I know.

Three arches connected by two lines. It's what Megan drew in the interrogation room. Putting these two things together leaves me dumbfounded. Moon takes my silence as a win.

He chuckles. "Hey, I'm not trying to rub it in, but it seems like maybe I'm a better investigator."

"A better investigator?" I say, "Thing is, I'm an FBI agent."

Moon pulls back his shoulders, looking me dead in the eye. "The good news is we have a prime suspect. That's something we didn't have last night. Last night all we had was a kid who'd been murdered. Now we have a motive. Now we have a lead."

"And what are you going to do with that information?" I ask him, the tension in the room palpable.

I look over at Howie, who's unusually quiet. His sidekick Cruz stands there with her arms crossed. Everyone seems to be on Moon's side. It's not that I don't want his team following the sheriff, but it seems so improbable that Willow had anything to do with this.

"I really appreciate your assistance," Moon tells me, "but we'll be handling the investigation from this point forward."

"What are you really saying?" I ask.

"I'm telling you, you're welcome to stick around in Olympia, but that we don't need you here at the station."

"Look, I can help. I've got people looking for Megan's mother right now.""

"Right. You told me that in the cafeteria. What was her name again?"

"Sandy. Last known address was Capitol Hill in Seattle, but we don't have a location on her currently."

"All right," Moon says. "Well, I'll let you know when we find her, not that it should have any bearing on the current situation."

The confidence that he'll be finding the mother before I do sends more than irritation up my spine. It infuriates me. Moon opens another box, grabbing a book from it before he heads out of the office, presumably to conduct the investigation with Willow Grace, interrogating her on his own.

I look at Howie. "What the hell is that about?" I ask.

Howie shrugs. "You didn't see the cabin, Holt. The kids' prints were all over it. Their clothes, their shoes, their books."

I run a hand over my jaw. "And what was in the padlocked room?"

Howie points to the boxes that are now dotting the office. "All this shit," he says. "And Holt, I've got to tell you. None of it looks good for Willow Grace."

20 WILLOW GRACE

The room is overheated. I shove the sleeves of my sweater to my elbows and pull at the neck, trying to lower my body temperature. But I'm hot, sweaty, and uncomfortable, and I know exactly why. This room is small, intentionally so to make the interrogation process more powerful, and it's working. Whoever is going to be interrogating me hasn't even come in yet, and I feel like a nervous wreck.

I'm alone in the room, and I look around, scoping it out. There is a two-way mirror. I know there are cameras, but I've never been in the position of being in a room like this before, waiting to be questioned for criminal activities.

Have I committed crimes? Sure, but not the kind they're after.

I look at my watch, staring as the seconds tick by, one after the next, minutes passing. They're trying to make me uncomfortable, and it's working way too well.

Finally, the door opens. I was lost in thought, and it startles me. I sit up straight, my hands on the table as if I'm waiting for my palms to be pressed against a lie detector that's not there. I swallow, parched, wanting water. There's none to be found.

Sheriff Moon enters the room. The way he looks at me makes me feel vulnerable, like he knows things about me I haven't told anyone. He offers me a smile that I'm not expecting.

I need to get a grip – focus.

It is time to think like a psychologist. What's Moon's game here? First, he's going to try and warm me up. He wants to make me comfortable, which if that's the case, why does he have the room so damn hot?

"So," he says. "We've met. As a refresher, I'm Sheriff Moon, and you're Willow Grace."

I narrow my eyes. "That's true," I agree. I try to keep my wry smile at bay.

He chuckles. "All right, so you're funny."

"Not usually called that, but I'll take it," I say, watching each of his movements with care, wanting clues as to what he is after with me.

He sets a legal pad and book on the table. The pad is on top, and I can't tell what title he's carrying or why. He pulls a pen out of his shirt pocket, clicking it back and forth, as fast as the seconds ticking by on my watch.

"I want to get a few facts," he says.

"Good," I say. "I'm happy to help in any way I can. I want Megan's kidnapper and her brother's killer to be found. I'm here to help," I say plainly, honestly.

He looks at me with disbelief, mouth parting slightly. "I'm mostly interested in the basics," he begins, starting the interview. "What were you doing at the time Megan arrived at your home?"

"I was making coffee," I say.

"Coffee," he repeats. "And what time was that?"

"It was just after five. I hadn't slept well." I pause. Do I want to tell him about the motion sensors going off in the middle of the night? Will that make me look more suspicious or less? I swallow, tugging again at the neck of my shirt. "I hadn't slept well, so I was making coffee. I woke up early. I usually do, but this was extra early, barely five. I had just poured water into the pot. Before I even added it to the maker, I heard a knock."

"A knock?" he asks. "That's what you heard?"

"Well, not at first. At first, I heard the motion sensors in my house go off, so it startled me. I spilled water all over myself, and then when I checked the panel to see what had made the sensors activate, I heard a knock. She must have knocked three, four times."

"You took that long to answer your door?"

"Well, I wasn't sure who it was, and I was a little startled."

"Why were you startled?"

"Because of the sensors," I repeat, knowing he won't understand.

Unless he has reason to fear the outside world, why would someone feel compelled to put alarm bells all over their home?

I have never had to justify my lifestyle before, and I don't like being forced to explain myself.

I can do my job on campus with the students just fine. I don't get bent out of shape with everything going on around me because I feel safe there. There are security guards, there are protocols. I don't feel threatened on campus. In my home, though, alone in the middle of nowhere, I do.

Not for the first time, I wonder if I have made a mistake by isolating myself. Maybe a better move would've been purchasing a condo in a large complex with neighbors on all sides of me. But I know why I didn't do that; I didn't want to be boxed in.

Not anymore.

I wanted to be free, which is why sitting in this room at this moment is so difficult. Why I am sweating so much, why my words feel jumbled. Small, windowless spaces, where I am not in control, are my worst nightmare.

"All right," he says. "And tell me about your work."

"I'm a professor."

"Of what?"

"Of psychology," I say.

"And do you do anything else besides your teaching?"

"Yeah, I offer private therapy too. Not so often, just in my area of expertise. Every once in a while I have a situation where--"

"Where you can what?" He presses me. "What's your expertise?"

"Didn't we already talk about this?" I ask.

"A bit, but not on camera."

I exhale, resigned. "Look, I've done a lot of research in cult behavior, cult psychology. How people are drawn to groups and are changed because of them."

A smile curls on his lips, and I feel like he's itching for something, looking for me to fall in a pit. I don't know what that pit is, though, and why he'd want me to fall. Isn't his job to help everyone soar? Why else would you want to be in law enforcement?

"I'm wondering about your security systems. They're quite extensive for a cabin worth a few hundred thousand dollars. We're not talking about some mansion that you need to protect."

"No, it's not the property or something lavish that I'm trying to keep secure. It's just me."

"You? You're that big of a threat?"

"Wait," I say, pausing. "You were at my house, weren't you?" My eyes flick up to the video camera in the corner of the room, and all I can hope is that Holt is there watching, taking this in, as curious about Moon's line of questioning as I am. What is he trying to get at?

Moon pulls something from his pocket and unfolds it. I know what it is before he explains. I saw Megan draw it when she was sitting with Holt earlier. I watched her pull the red crayon from the box and draw this on the white piece of paper he is holding.

"Have you seen this before? This symbol?" he asks.

"I don't think I have. Not before today, at least, when I saw Megan draw it earlier."

He frowns. "I didn't realize you were watching the entirety of her questioning."

"Yeah, I was. Holt had brought me here, and I wanted to make sure she was all right."

"That was highly inappropriate," he says.

"Deputy Thomas knew I was there, and Howie too. I wasn't doing anything wrong. I would've left if someone had told me to, but-"

"No," he says. "It's fine. You hadn't seen it before though?"

I shake my head no. "I don't think so, but a part of me wonders if maybe I have?" To be certain, I need to go through my things at home.

"And this," he says, pulling something out that's tucked in his notepad. It's a glossy 8-by-10 photograph. The photo is of a blood-stained knife, and on the handle of it, the same symbol is carved.

"Where did you get this? Was this the murder weapon for Megan's brother?"

Moon looks at me hard. His eyes glaring, nostrils flared. "I wanted you to tell me about what it takes to condition a captive's mind."

"A captive's mind?" I ask. "Am I being questioned as an expert or a suspect?" I feel a spotlight on me and as a psychologist, I know guilty people feel this way, an overwhelming floodlight on them during an interrogation, during a questioning when they have done something wrong. And I know it's making me more nervous. Logically, I know I need to stop, that I need to calm down. But my anxiety is at an all-time high, and I know that it's making me look more and more guilty.

Every time I shove the shirt sleeves up to my elbows, every time I pull at the neck of my sweater, every time I pull my hair into my hand, twisting it at the nape of my neck, I know it makes me look guilty, as if I have something to hide.

I don't.

"As a suspect," he clarifies. "Not as an expert, not now. But I can tell this is making you very uneasy, isn't it?" He pulls the book out from underneath the legal pad. He slides it across the table.

I swallow. I know this book well since I wrote it. Tending the Flock: A Conditioning of Captives. "Where did you get this?" But the question is ridiculous because I know exactly where it came from. It came from my cabin, in my personal library that's locked away in my secret room behind a padlock.

Now I understand the look Moon has been giving me and why. He must have seen everything in that room and made an assumption. He thinks I'm obsessive, as opposed to an expert. He thinks I did something to hurt Megan instead of doing my best to make her feel safe in the short time we had together.

"How did you get this? Why did you go into my home?"

Moon leans back. His demeanor is cockier now, and he shrugs. "Well, I certainly didn't get it out of the public library."

My eyes narrow. I bite my bottom lip. None of this makes sense. I know the truth, but Moon is trying to bend it. "I don't know what you're getting at," I say. "You think I did something to lure Megan to my house? Why would I do that? It was storming last night, pouring down rain. I slept terribly. She shows up at my house--"

"Oh, I know that's your story, but I'm not so certain that's the whole story."

Aggravated, I feel like I could scream. Instead, I press my hands into fists, regaining control over myself. "I need to speak with Agent Holt," I tell him.

Moon pulls the book back toward himself, flipping through the pages slowly, excruciatingly slowly as if trying to taunt me. Without looking at me, he flippantly says, "That's not possible. Holt is no longer a part of this investigation."

My heart sinks at the words. He's been taken off this case. Why? Then it dawns on me.

There's only one reason. They think they found the killer.

Moon flips to a section of the book and turns it back toward me. The chapter heading reads, "When the flock goes astray." He runs his finger down the page and says to me, "What is it you say in your book? There are two options: reconditioning or exile."

A feeling of desperation rises within me. I feel myself rambling, trying to fit in more words that are necessary so he understands me, believes me. Overexplaining that I have nothing to do with Megan and her brother.

"Ask Holt," I plead. "He can tell you I was taking care of that little girl. I made sure she got cleaned up, took a bath. I combed her hair. I made her pancakes. I was--"

"Care or reconditioning, which one is it, Willow Grace?"

I stammer, and when I don't find words fast enough, Moon continues. "There were no prints on the knife, but plenty of blood. Explain that."

"Where did you even find that?" I ask. "It couldn't have been in my home."

Moon doesn't hesitate. "It was in the cabin, along with all of your other cult memorabilia. Items of the children, your personal effects."

I know how this all looks, like I am obsessive, like I am a freak, and I can't fathom how all of it got there, but I know I've been set up. My mind reels as I try to put pieces together, but nothing fits. Moon, though, already has his own theory, and he has no problem letting me know it.

"Here's what I think," he says, leaning back in his chair. "I think you are a disturbed woman. You've gone to a great length to live a reclusive life. Sure, you have a good job, stable income, but that's what, a few hours a day. The rest of the time you live in the woods. You didn't have any children. You couldn't have any children, so you decided to take them."

"No," I say. "That's not the truth."

"What part? You can't have kids or-"

"No, I can't have children, but I didn't take any. I-"

"I did some digging," he says, cutting me off. "You were living in Seattle for a very brief time about seven years ago, about the same time these two children went missing. And then poof, you are gone. They're gone. Off the grid and living out here in an isolated cabin with an intricate security system."

I press my lips together, willing myself to stay quiet because I'm terrified that anything I say right now will only worsen the situation. I know if I expose the real reason for leaving Seattle, it will only cast more suspicion on me. And right now, that's the last thing I need.

Moon adds, "We can find out a lot more about you. Hell, maybe we'll learn more once we get you fingerprinted and processed."

I shake my head, and even though the room is way too hot, I feel the blood draining from my face. "Why wouldn't I have helped? Ask Holt, he was there. He was at my cabin. He saw me with Megan."

Moon calmly runs a hand over his jaw. "He also said she had been with you for a couple of hours by the time he arrived, and yet in that time you made no effort to call the police. It makes me think maybe she'd been there a hell of a lot longer than that. Which tracks with the fact we found her clothing, her shoes, her belongings, all in your cabin along with her brother's."

"What?" I'm stunned by his revelation. "It's not possible. Someone planted them. Someone is trying to frame me--"

"Listen," he says, cutting me off once and for all. He stands, pushing away from the table. "I want to ask you something, Willow Grace, what does exile mean to you?"

I look at him, my heart pounding, but he doesn't even wait a beat.

Instead, he offers, "According to your book, it can come in many forms, excommunication or death. It seems in the case of Kevin Talbot, you chose the latter. All I can say is thankfully Agent Holt found you in time."

His words slice right through me. He thinks I killed Kevin. He thinks I've been holding Megan captive. With his hand on the doorknob, he turns back to me. "I want to serve an arrest warrant to you, but that's not going to happen. Legal problems might arise from holding you against your will. But what I am going to do is let you know that a warrant for your arrest will be forthcoming. Be ready for it."

My jaw drops. "Is that a threat?"

He sneers. "Take it however you like."

Anger is rising in me as I look at him. I'm not scared, not panicking. Just pissed. Moon is one hell of an ass.

"I need an attorney," I say. I'm owed that.

Moon gives me a grin of satisfaction. "You better make sure it's a good one, because, Willow Grace, you're going to need it."

21 WILLOW GRACE

After my interrogation with Moon, I run into Holt in the hallway. I've been cleared to leave the station, but my vibration is high; I feel like I could explode. The entire conversation with Moon has left me so insanely frustrated.

Holt looks at me with concern, eyebrows knit together. "You okay?"

I give an awkward laugh. "I've been better," I say.

He runs a hand over his jaw, looking at me. "Can I give you a ride back home?"

"Actually, yes. Thanks," I say. "I just need to get my coat and my purse. I'll be a sec?"

"No problem. I can wait."

I enter the waiting room and retrieve my items, pulling on the coat, the purse over my shoulder. I check my phone for the first time all day. No missed calls, but I'm not surprised. I don't have much of a social life. Still, I'm surprised at the time. It's five o'clock in the evening. I've been at the station for hours, and I'm exhausted.

When we walk out of the station, it's dark and gray. Not because the sun has set, but because the rainstorm rolling through Thurston

County for the last twenty-four hours hasn't quite left. I pull the hood up on my jacket, and Holt does the same.

"Damn," he says, "I don't think I'll ever get used to the weather out here on the West Coast."

"Where are you from?" I ask.

He smiles over at me. "Midwest. Born and raised."

"Yeah? Whereabouts?"

"Oklahoma City. You ever been there?"

"Not even once," I answer.

"Where'd you grow up?" he asks. I lick my lips, wishing I hadn't fallen into this line of conversation. Usually I do my best to avoid it, but I'm off my game, especially after the day I've had.

"I grew up outside of Seattle," I say.

He nods. "I'm living in the heart of the city now."

"You like it?" I ask.

He shrugs. "The city is full of tech bros. Not really my type."

"What is your type?" I ask as he uses a key fob to unlock his vehicle.

I slide into the passenger seat as he sits in the driver's. He turns on the engine and presses the seat warmers for both of us. "My type," he says. "Hmm, I prefer people who don't lead with their accomplishments. How about that?"

I nod. "Yeah, I like that too. With my line of work in academia, some people always want to make sure everyone knows the prizes they've won and the awards they've received. It's all about recognition."

"And that's not you?" Holt asks me.

I shake my head, buckling up. "No, not at all."

"You don't like to talk about yourself?"

"Not really, though it seems like I did plenty of it today. Though none of it did me any good."

I lean back into the headrest as Holt reverses the car and pulls onto the main road.

"You had a hell of a time back there, huh, with Moon?"

"That's one way to put it. Moon told me you're off the case. Apparently they already have their prime suspect."

He looks over at me. Our gazes meet, and we hold it for a beat too long. I swallow, looking forward out the window.

"It was brutal," I offer. "I think mostly because I was not expecting it. Usually I plan things out in my life pretty well. If I have a plan, if I know what I'm doing, I'm okay. That's why teaching works so well," I explain. "I make the lesson plan. There's never much in the way of surprises."

"And you live alone too, which means you're kind of the king of your own castle."

"Exactly," I say, appreciating how he seems to get it. ""What about you, do you live alone?"

He nods, looking over at me. "Yep. Ever since my ex-girlfriend split."

"How long ago was that?"

"Four years."

"That's pretty long."

"Yeah. Do you have a partner?" he asks nonchalantly.

"No," I reply, thinking how Malcolm wishes that weren't the case.

"How come? You seem pretty, smart and you're successful at what you do."

"I could say the same for you."

He chuckles. "So you're saying I'm pretty?"

I laugh. "I thought this was going to be more awkward than it is," I tell him.

"You want some awkward silence in the car as I drive?" he asks. "Because I usually do my best to avoid that."

"I noticed that you're pretty chill," I tease, surprised at how easy it is to be in a car with a man I have just met. Usually that stresses me out.

"Are you hungry?" he asks.

"I could eat." It is the first time since the pancakes this morning I have thought about food.

"I saw a burger joint on the way to the station this morning."

"That place is pretty good. High Five?"

"Yeah, that's the one." A few minutes later we pull into the drive-through and order cheeseburgers and fries. I splurge for a chocolate shake, and Holt gets a diet coke.

"The caffeine might keep you up," I warn.

He chuckles as he pulls out of the parking lot and back onto the highway. "Like you should talk. That shake is sixteen ounces of pure sugar."

"Fair," I acknowledge. "Though, I'm hoping the grease and sugar makes me crash. I'm exhausted. I slept like hell last night."

"Yeah?" He looks over at me. "I'm sorry."

"Well, you did too. You're running on fumes, right? You didn't get any sleep at all?"

"Nope. I came right from Seattle yesterday. I haven't even checked into the motel yet."

"In that case, thanks for driving me back. I know it's keeping you from getting some shuteye."

"I'll sleep soon enough. Hell, I'm off the case. I have nothing going on."

I laugh at his ability to make light of a tough situation. Digging into the paper bag I grab some French fries, grateful for the company. We eat as he drives, and the familiarity that passes between us surprises me. I wonder what it is about Holt that makes him so easy to talk to. However he grew up, it must have been very different from me.

"You know," I muse, the closer we get to my house, "Megan's going to need some intensive therapy. I'm really worried about her. Whatever she's gone through, it's done a number on her."

Holt seems to pause, looking at me. "You care about her?"

"I care about what happens next for her, for her brother. He deserves justice for what happened to him."

Holt takes a drink of diet coke. "Well, Moon will be working on getting an arrest warrant passed through a prosecutor and judge. The best thing you can do now is get yourself a good lawyer."

"Moon mentioned that," I remark, unwrapping the burger.

"Heed his advice. You shouldn't even discuss the case with me, because anything you say can later be held against you."

"Is that a Miranda Rights warning or something?" I ask, now very familiar with court proceedings.

"Not per se, but I mean it, Willow. I don't want you to say something you're going to regret."

"Well, there's nothing to say about Megan that's going to get me in trouble. I didn't kidnap those kids. I didn't kill Kevin. I had nothing to do with this. I met the girl this morning. That girl who was fragile and shaking, who was soaking wet and hungry." I shake my head, shoving fries in my mouth.

So frustrated, I don't know how to explain myself. "I know what Moon must have seen at my house," I try to find the right words. "All that stuff about cults and religions and creepy situations that have gone on throughout the country. I get it – it looks strange. But none of that ties me to wanting to brainwash a little girl and her brother. You've seen my cabin., the property. I couldn't have kept two kids there for seven years."

"I get what you're saying," Holt says more calmly than I'd like. "But I also know the evidence that Moon has presented."

"You're implying you think I'm guilty?"

"No, I'm telling you there's a case being built, and you need a lawyer to help you get out of it."

When we get to my cabin, I thank him for dinner and for the ride. "I'd say anytime, but I'm not sure when I'm going to see you again," he tells me.

"Well now it's awkward," I murmur climbing out of the vehicle.

"It doesn't have to be, Willow. Maybe our paths will cross again."

"I wouldn't be opposed to that," I smile, my hand on the passenger door.

"Me neither. And listen, good luck with everything. You can always call if you need the help of an FBI agent."

I laugh. "I appreciate it. I hope you can find Megan's mother. She deserves to be reunited with her daughter."

Holt looks at me for a long time, as if wanting to say more. The overhead lighting in the car illuminates his face, giving his features a soft glow, and I force myself to look away.

"Uh, speaking of," he says. A text message comes through the phone that's tethered to the console of his car.

"What?" I pause.

"I just received word that the mother has been located in Tacoma."

I press my lips together. It's not that I'm sad; I want Megan to be back with her mom, but I feel scared, like there's a heaviness to the situation I didn't realize before.

Probably because I hadn't been the suspect in a murder investigation.

22 WILLOW GRACE

It's painful to walk inside my cabin. The moment I close the door behind me, tears fill my eyes. I'm not a crier. I do my best to keep strong, but right now it's hard, because when I look at this place I created to be my safe haven, my cocoon from the world at large, I only see destruction.

The pieces of my life I have so carefully built are destroyed and in disarray. And it's not just throw pillows on the floor and blankets tossed aside. It's all the papers flung about, all the cupboard doors swung open, all the drawers pulled out, like I'm exposed. Vulnerable in a way I haven't been since I left home.

I wipe the tears from my eyes, not wanting to be weak. This cabin, while ripped apart, is also my home. I don't need to fall apart – not yet. Right now, I can put my place back together. All is not lost even if it feels that way.

And while I'm alone in this cabin, I haven't been arrested. I'm not being questioned in an interrogation room. I'm not being grilled by an officer whose intent is to harm me.

Right now, I am safe. I set down my purse and take off my jacket, slip off my shoes, and pace my home, addressing one area at a time.

Shutting the drawers and cabinets in the kitchen. Pushing the chairs back under the table, standing the salt and pepper shakers, wondering why on earth someone would've knocked them over so carelessly. Have the people who searched my home been that careless about me? And if they were so careless about this house, how are they treating the case? Deep in my bones I worry anyone could walk into my house and treat it so callously. This place that I painstakingly put together.

I never wanted to simply live in a cabin, I wanted a home.

The rug that runs down the hallway, I picked it out with thoughtfulness, wanting my feet to touch an extra cushioned carpet every time I walked from my bedroom to the bathroom. Because when I was a child, I didn't have such a luxury. It was concrete, bare feet, ice cold everything. The hugs from the adults, the confinement in which I was kept, the porridge for breakfast and dinner. Nothing about where I grew up felt like home.

And even though I live here all by myself without a family, I still did my best to make this place a nurturing environment for me to grow. Even now, as a thirty-five-year-old woman, I'm still learning how to care for my childlike heart.

That's why I was happy to make Megan pancakes and a fruit salad this morning. It's why I combed her hair with tenderness and made sure she was clean. Every time I can do those simple acts of kindness for someone else, I heal a part of my inner child, a part of me that has been forgotten for so long. The parts of me that were never there at all.

When I walk into the guest room, my heart beats hard. The mattress is pulled up, the blankets and pillows on the floor. The closet is swung wide open. I remember Sheriff Moon telling me that the children's items were here, but the closet is nearly empty, except for some of my sweaters that I keep there for the winter and a couple of bins of Christmas decorations. There's no clothing belonging to any children. I realize it must have all been confiscated.

How did they get here in the first place? Someone did that.

Someone made a choice to take those items and put them here, wanting me to take the blame.

After I reassemble the guest room, I notice the deadbolt on the floor in the hall by the kitchen. My private space has been completely dismantled. This is more painful than the other spaces – this is my space where I work to find meaning out of heartbreak, where I try to make peace with the cruelty of the world.

The door that was supposed to be padlocked is swung wide open, and inside I see papers ripped and discarded. The corkboard that had been filled with ideas for my next book -- about brainwashing practices – has all been taken down and removed.

The police think I was brainwashing Megan and Kevin, that all this time I've been plotting in this room, to hurt innocent children.

Why would I go to such extremes? Brainwashing the kids, meanwhile writing books about it and selling them to publishers? That level of risk is unheard of. Maybe they think I needed real life research, but if that's what they think, they have it all wrong. I didn't need kids to kidnap in order to understand the mechanics of cults brainwashing people.

My childhood taught me that, if it taught me anything at all.

It's devastating to see what's happened here. How the pieces I have so carefully brought together for my research have been so quickly destroyed.

Eventually I need to get those boxes of evidence back. It's all the research for my next book.

When I walk into my bedroom, I immediately look in the dresser drawer where I kept my gun. I placed it here before I left with Holt this morning. Now it's missing. Of course it is. It must have been confiscated by the police along with so much else.

I run my hand over the now empty drawer. On the wooden bottom of the dresser drawer, there are flakes of dried blood. This must be where they found the knife. My stomach rolls, and I regret that cheeseburger I ate on the way here.

I feel nauseous as I begin to fully realize there is a strong case against me.

As much as I try to grapple with this, it's impossible to understand why someone would have planted the evidence against me. I have no enemies at work. Besides the people at trivia night, I don't know anyone besides the people at my job. Why would someone do this to me? Why would they hurt me, or worse – hurt these children?

Tears prick my eyes again as I walk to the security camera system to see if there's anything there that would prove my innocence or show me who came in and set this trap into motion. But all the cameras are offline. The police took my entire recording system, which is the biggest blow of all.

Tonight, I won't have any motion detectors to activate to make me feel safe. How will I be able to close my eyes and get rest? No, all night I will be on guard, scared, maybe more terrified than I have been before, because whoever planted this evidence might want to hurt me.

They might come back and do something worse, not just plant a knife here, but use a knife *on me*. There will be no questions; they're going to want to shut me up. The reality of what's happening is overwhelming.

I move to the fireplace, adding kindling and logs to the hearth, striking a match, watching it go up in flames. Sitting in front of the fire, I wrap my arms around my legs, pulling my knees to my chin. I'm trying not to tremble. I'm trying not to shake. But as I sit in front of the fire, warming myself, looking for comfort, it's not lost on me that this is the same spot where Megan tried to comfort herself this morning.

Maybe I am more like that little girl than I realize.

23 PAXTON HOLT

INSTEAD OF STAYING at the motel in Thurston County, I head back to my place in Seattle. I need a good night's rest, and I'm not going to get it tossing and turning at a motel in a town where I'm no longer wanted.

In the morning, I work out, shave, and get myself together before I head into the office in downtown Seattle. I'm trying to shake the fact that I failed to find the two missing children seven years ago. But it feels nearly impossible. The weight is heavy on my shoulders.

Now one of them is dead, which is a burden I can't ignore. Not everyone would understand. I remember the way their mother looked, tortured, and in so much pain for not knowing where her children were. I remember feeling so incapable at my job when I couldn't locate them. Now one of them is dead, and there's nothing that can change that.

When I enter the office, my boss Tamara walks over to my cubicle to congratulate me.

"That's impressive that you were able to locate the missing girl. I read the file, and I'm so happy, I mean, about her. My condolences, of course, for the boy. Did you get a chance to speak with the girl at all?"

"Not much," I say. "I tried to interview her, but she wasn't that responsive. Speaking of which, The girl is really going to need extensive therapy. Willow Grace, the woman who found her in the woods, she's a psychologist, and she really impacted me when she said how important it is that this girl gets services."

"Of course, I know social services is already working on a unification process."

"Really?" I ask. "So the mom is clean enough to be with her daughter?"

"Sounds like she was in a halfway house last year. She recently transitioned to a place of her own. She's been clean for a chunk of time. So, the next step is to reunite the kid with her mom. The program the mom's working for has her set up in an apartment that can accommodate both of them."

"Wow," I say. "I mean, I guess that's the dream, right? That a family can come back together."

It's not lost on me that it's not the whole family, that some people will never return to where they belong.

"When the reunification happens with the social worker, can I be present?" I ask.

Tamara runs a hand over her arm. "I don't see why not. After all, you were involved with the case seven years ago, plus you were the one who found her. Do you think she feels safe with you?"

"I'd say so. I bought her donuts."

Tamara grins. "Well, that always helps with a ten-year-old, huh?"

"I suppose so." I shake my head, thinking of Megan. "She is pretty special, and hella tough. Been through hell as far as I can tell." I just wish I knew the reason why ... there is so much to understand and none of it seems connected to Willow. I hate that Thurston County is pinning anything on her. There is no way she would hurt those kids.

Tamara nods. "Well, I'll text you the address when I get it from the social worker. I think they planned the reunification for eleven this morning. The girl's on her way now from Thurston County to Tacoma. The mom moved there from Seattle a few years back."

"All right," I say, feeling hopeful for Megan and her mom. I know my relationship with my mom was rocky at best. And we never got our second chance. Maybe Megan will get the one she deserves. "I appreciate it."

"Of course. And, Holt, don't let the stuff you haven't accomplished take away from the things you have."

"Easier said than done," I tell her.

"That's fair," she says. "It doesn't mean it's any less true."

24 WILLOW GRACE

I ALWAYS ENJOY GOING to work, and today is no exception. I'm craving the outdoors, a chance to stretch my legs, to breathe in the deep, fresh air. And most importantly, impart more of what I have gleaned over my years as a psychologist to my new students.

Finally, the rain has stopped, and the ground isn't as wet as it was yesterday. I pull on a pair of hiking boots and Levi's, a polar fleece, and I braid my hair down my back. I fill my thermos with coffee and head to my car. I have an eight o'clock lecture and everyone knows to meet at the same trailhead where I typically begin each of my classes. Once I park, I hustle through campus, chugging my coffee as I go.

Even though my name wasn't released to the press about everything that happened yesterday, I feel eyes upon me. It is as if people know I was in an interrogation room for hours, that Sheriff Moon was asking me questions about a situation I had no part in.

I look away, not wanting anyone's attention, not wanting any focus. It's always been one of my greatest fears -- being found. But right now, I feel like I've already been caught.

As I get to the trailhead, there is a ping on my phone alerting me there's a new email in my inbox. I click it open realizing it's from Dean Clarence.

We would like to inform you the 8:00 AM lecture on cult conditioning has been canceled.

The email has gone out to all my students.

I look up, seeing that no one is at the trailhead. That's surprising. At least I would've expected Charlotte to be here extra early. I close the lid of my coffee thermos and tuck it in my backpack before walking across campus to the dean's office.

Maybe there was an emergency or some issue on campus I hadn't been aware of.

Once I get to Dean Clarence's office, he's busy on a phone call. I watch through the glass door window. He rubs his face, clearly stressed.

He's shaking his head and taking a few notes on a pad of paper in front of him. When he hangs up, he gestures for me to enter.

I shut the door and take a seat opposite his desk. "I got an email," I say, holding my phone up as if that is proof. "My class was canceled. I don't know what it's about; is something going on?"

Clarence exhales. He's an older man who's always been fair to me. I have no reason not to trust him now. He looks tired, though, worn out in ways he shouldn't be. It's only eight in the morning. He should be bright-eyed and bushy-tailed this time of day.

"Thing is, Willow, I got a call from the sheriff's office. He told me you were a suspect in an ongoing investigation."

My face falls, not having expected that, and I realize, what was I thinking? If they think I'm a murder suspect, of course, I can't be teaching students.

"Well, that may be true, but everything you've heard isn't right. I didn't do anything. It's all been a giant misunderstanding. Someone set me up."

"Listen," Clarence says, "I can only go on what I've been given by the sheriff. I don't like this any more than you do."

"No, I'm pretty sure I like this less than you do," I say, "It's my actual life, Clarence. The sheriff is trying to pin murder on me. They think I've been holding a pair of kids hostage in my cabin for the last seven years!"

"Look," he says, shaking his head, his fingers on his temples. "I just got off the phone with the school's president and by policy, all of your classes have been suspended in full until further notice."

"What are you talking about? I haven't been charged with anything. You won't even let me teach?"

"If there's an ongoing criminal investigation, there are grounds for immediate dismissal, Willow. We're doing you a favor by just pausing them."

I see. I'm being punished because Sheriff Moon can't find a real suspect for this murder investigation. Great.

My entire body tenses. All those years of therapy where I was working so hard on myself to be grounded, to be centered, to stay Zen, I feel like they're slipping away so fast. It's like the moment I'm thrust back into a traumatic situation, I revert to my old patterns of behavior.

I'm a psychologist. I know better than this. I try to take a deep breath, inhale and exhale, but all I can think as I'm doing it is that I must look crazy to the dean.

"Willow, you've been a shining star in our psychology program; the college is lucky to have you. I convinced the president to hold on a termination. Suspension is better for everyone, especially for you."

"And what about my students? They're just going to miss class for however long or are you transferring them somewhere else?"

"There's no transfer happening. Not now. Let's hope this will be cleared up by the end of the week."

My face falls at the reality. "I sure hope so."

"Well, in the meantime," Clarence says, "I suggest you get the best defense attorney you can find."

I press my lips together, swallowing my bitter anger. For so long, I was a victim. I fought to change that, to get myself in a healthy place, to go to college and grad school, and become a writer. I fought to break the cycle.

Now I feel like everything I worked for is literally slipping away, and all those things are gone.

What do I have left? A lonely life in a cabin -- or worse, a life in prison.

"I know exactly what lawyer to speak with," I say, standing up and walking to the door. "Thank you, Clarence, for not firing me. And I promise you this -- I will clear my name, and I will find the real killer."

25 PAXTON HOLT

I'M WAITING on the sidewalk outside of the apartment building where Megan's mother lives when I see Megan and a social worker walking toward me. Megan is talking to the social worker, and that alone is a relief. Looks like she started opening up. I'm not sure about what but saying anything at all is an improvement to her odds.

When she sees me, though, she slows her walk, and her face turns to a frown. When they reach me, I introduce myself.

"I'm Paxton Holt. I work for the FBI agency downtown. I'm the one who helped bring Megan home."

The social worker reaches out her hand and shakes mine. "I'm Lucy. It's nice to meet you. Megan, can you say hello to Agent Holt?"

"Hi," she says. Her voice is soft, and she won't meet my eyes. "Do you know where Willow is?" she asks.

With that question, her voice is clearer. I look at Lucy, unsure how to proceed.

Lucy speaks for me. "She's in Olympia. Remember, she's a teacher there. She's a professor at the college. So, she's probably at work today, and what's great is everybody has big, busy lives to lead, just like you. You're going to be in school soon and learning and experiencing all sorts of new things."

Lucy gives her a bright smile that's unreturned by Megan.

I swallow, watching the exchange. Both alarmed at the fact that Megan wants to be with Willow instead of her own mother, yet also aware of Willow's calming presence.

I felt that too when I was driving her home last night. There's something about that woman, and I know it isn't evil.

"We're going to go inside now, Megan," Lucy says. "And meet your mom. I know she's really excited to see you."

"This is where she lives?" Megan asks, eyeing the building warily.

Lucy nods. "Yep. She lives here now, and the place has two bedrooms, so the timing's great. You can get settled into a new home together." Lucy turns to me. "Her name is Valerie."

Megan doesn't seem to know how to react. She just follows Lucy and me into the building. We take the elevator to the third floor, and Lucy locates apartment number 34. She knocks. A moment later a thin, petite woman with cropped blue hair opens the door.

She's already crying. "Oh my God!" she gasps, reaching for Megan, wrapping her arms around her shoulders. "My baby. You're home. You're home. You're alive."

She presses her hands to Megan's cheeks, searching her gaze. Megan is frozen like a deer in headlights. She doesn't say a word. Her eyes flicker between Lucy and me.

Her mom doesn't seem to notice. "You're so big! Look at you. You're almost as tall as me. Come in. Come in," she says. "Now don't worry, Megan. We're going to get all new things. Okay? I'm going to get a new couch, and I already got a bed. My neighbor brought one in for you and there's two bedrooms here, so it's perfect. Just you and me, and there's a bathroom and a kitchen. Do you want to see it?"

She's talking a mile a minute as if trying to overcompensate for the things that she hasn't been able to provide for Megan over the last seven years.

"And I got some of your favorite foods," she adds. "I remember when you were little you loved red apples. You didn't like the green ones. Do you still like red apples?"

Megan is crying now, tears rolling down her cheeks and her mom seems to interpret that as tenderness. But even though I've only known Megan for a day, I can register it's not a soft heart toward her mom that she's feeling. It's fear.

She's overwhelmed.

I sat with her in that interrogation room long enough yesterday to know there is a depth to this girl. She's holding a lot in, a lot back, and none of it has to do with her mother. I'm not surprised. She was abducted when she was three years old. She has no recollection of this woman, red apples or green. And whatever she's been experiencing the last seven years, heavy brainwashing had to be present.

She's scared to speak, to say her truth, to say any of it.

Lucy and I take a seat on the couch, and Valerie sits opposite us. Megan doesn't seem to know where to stand.

Lucy does her job and fills in the gaps. "Hey, why don't you take a seat in that chair?" she suggests. "Next to your mom." She points to a rocking chair. Everything looks secondhand, like it's been here a long time as tenants come and go.

Megan sits and begins rocking in the old wooden chair. It reminds me of the way she was rocking yesterday morning when I discovered her in Willow's cabin.

"So what do you like to do?" Valerie asks Megan. "What are your hobbies? Your favorite color? What's your favorite movie? I want to know everything. I missed you so much, and I have so much to say. I'm so sorry, but I'm also so happy you're here. And Kevin. Oh, poor Kevin. I heard that he..." At this, she starts to cry.

Lucy hands her tissues from her purse, and Valerie wipes her eyes, blowing her nose. "I know I'm not supposed to get into Kevin today. I know. I know," she cries.

Megan rocks faster in the chair. She's triggered by her brother's name or by her mother's emotion. I wish Willow were here to help me identify what's going on with this child. Lucy seems more worried about the mother, and I understand why.

We need to keep mom stable.

She looks clean now, but I've been around addiction long enough to know that it's a slippery slope. My mom was an addict. That's why I was so hell-bent on leaving Oklahoma City as soon as I could. I knew if I stayed, I'd be on the same path as everyone else in my family.

Drinking and using, working dead-end jobs, and unhappy with everything until they died. I wanted more. I want more for Megan too, for her mom even.

But I wonder if it's possible. My mom couldn't stop popping pills, and eventually it killed her. I swallow, suddenly feeling hot in this cramped apartment that needs to be deep cleaned.

"We can start learning about each other in the coming weeks," Lucy says. "The important thing right now is to gain a level of trust and understanding. Megan has had a hard time communicating her needs and desires right now, but we know that she's safe. She had a physical. Her body has not been harmed in any significant way, and the goal of the state service programs is to bring families together. You didn't lose custody of your daughter. Your daughter was abducted. The situation may be complicated, but it's not the same as a child being brought back to a family after being in foster care. Megan was kidnapped, and she has a long road of recovery ahead of her. She wasn't accessing services the last seven years like you have been able to. Do you understand that?" Lucy asks Valerie. "Do you understand what I'm saying?"

Valerie nods, wiping the tears away. She reaches out for Megan's arm, squeezing it. "I'm just so happy you're here, baby, and I'm going to be strong. I'm going to be a good mama for you. You understand me? I will never let you down."

Lucy steps in again. "The thing is, it's really important to not make promises, especially ones that are hyperbole. We're all going to let each other down. That's a part of life, Valerie, and that doesn't mean we can't do our best moving forward, but we're also going to do our best to say words that are true. I'm going to be conducting regular visits here. I'll be back tomorrow morning, that's a scheduled one, but I'll also have unscheduled ones because my most important job right now is to ensure the wellbeing of the entire family."

Megan looks like she's going to hyperventilate. She's breathing so fast, rocking so hard.

"Megan? I ask. "Megan, are you okay? What do you need? Do you need some water?" I surprise myself by jumping in. Her own mother and social worker are here, but right now she's not talking to either of them.

She's lost in her own world.

I stand, moving toward the rocking chair and kneeling before it. I place my hands on the armrests, stopping the momentum. Megan seems surprised, blinking out of her panic attack.

"I'm sorry," she apologizes. "I'm sorry. I don't know. I don't know what's wrong with me. I'm just..."

"I know," I say. "It's been a long few days."

She wraps her arms around my neck, and the gesture takes my breath away. It's not anything I was expecting. When was the last time I got a hug from a ten-year-old? I can't even remember. So much of my life is consumed looking for bad guys, sometimes I forget I'm doing that work to protect the good ones.

Before I leave the apartment, I pull Lucy aside. "Willow Grace who took Megan in yesterday, she's a psychologist. Her advice was to get Megan extensive therapy to assist her healing process. Clearly, she's going through some stuff."

Lucy nods. "I know. It's already been arranged. She'll start with a counselor tomorrow, actually. It'll be wraparound services. Don't worry. Even when she gets into school, she's going to have professionals on her team. They'll be okay. Again, she's just lucky you found her."

"Right. Lucky," I say, the words ringing false.

I leave the apartment complex not feeling buoyed by the reunification. Instead, I feel deflated, like I've let someone down, like I've messed this all up. And like Megan is going to pay the ultimate price.

26 BENJAMIN SHAW

My bride Hannah finds me in my office. "Father," she says, "an officer is here to see you."

I frown. I wasn't expecting a visitor. It's the middle of the day, and I've been working on my lecture for tomorrow night's community gathering. We're going back to the basics, focusing on the principles of The Harmony, namely serenity and devotion.

There's no way to find harmony between a group of people unless we surrender our own selfish ambition and focus on devoting ourselves to helping one another, namely the women helping the men.

It is one of our key tenets and something I think some members of our congregation forget. Like Earl Dawson, who seems to forget that his job was not to take vengeance on Kevin Talbot. Instead, his job was to bring him back to the fold, to devote himself to whatever he must do to bring Kevin home safely.

Instead, he killed the boy, and now we have to cover up his mess.

"Would you like me to bring in some tea?" Hannah asks.

I shake my head. "No, we're fine." I walk to the front of the house and see the officer.

Earl is with him. He has a black eye and a scrape on his face. He's been through hell the last 24 hours, but it's a hell he deserves. It's the only way to truly reconcile his choices. He had to pay penance.

The officer nods at me. "Can we have a word?"

"Of course," I say. "Hannah let me know you were here."

"Pretty, young wife," the officer says. "Still trying to understand how you were able to reel her in."

I chuckle, looking over at Earl who follows us. Earl is terrified to get anything wrong, and he knows his job right now is to be supervised at all times.

The three of us go into my office, taking seats, me behind my desk. They both sit in simple, hand-constructed wooden chairs.

"Where do things stand now?" I ask.

The officer tells me the facts. "I got rid of the FBI agent. And that woman, Willow, who lives in the cabin not too far from here, will be arrested soon enough. I got a warrant for her. We searched her cabin. It's all good on that front. But I want to do everything by the book because I don't want us to get any blow back."

"And you think this woman Willow will be charged and convicted?"

"I don't see how not. The case is strong against her. Everyone at the department agrees."

"There's no doubt then, that she did it?"

"None that anyone can find. She has the motive, she has the means."

"And Megan, how is she?" I ask.

The officer looks over at Earl. "She'd be a lot better if she hadn't watched her brother get murdered."

Earl's jaw tightens at that. "I didn't mean... I didn't..."

"Don't," I interrupt. "Don't go there, Earl, no one wants to hear you talk right now."

"She's been returned to her mother," the officer tells me.

This is the last thing I wanted to hear. I pound my fist on my desk. "No, that's not where she belongs! She belongs with us. We are her family. We will bring Harmony to her life, not that addict. A mother who can't even take care of her. No. No. I've made promises to her family that she will come home. You've made promises too, haven't you, Earl?"

Rage flows through my veins, and I stalk to Earl, striking him across the face. "This is your fault, all of it."

His shoulders shake as he begins to sob.

"Why do you even have him in here?" the officer asks.

"Because I can't trust him out of my sight. Not right now."

The officer nods. His eyes have dark circles under them. It's like he hasn't slept. He looks torn up, a mess.

I've seen him like this before, stress overtaking him. His family life, his problems with the job and his supervisor.

But he needs to keep himself together right now in order to protect The Harmony, and so does Earl.

"I want to know when the girl will be returning to us -- her proper family," I say to the officer.

"I got a plan for that," he says. "It's already in the works. But Earl, I'm gonna need your help."

27 WILLOW GRACE

In my office, I gather my things. It's painful packing a box of files and books I might need over the next week or longer. Thinking about it being longer makes my chest grow tight, fear winding up my throat.

I can't go back there to a life where I felt trapped. I couldn't live in a prison, not well, at least. This office is claustrophobic enough, and living in a cell would remind me so much of things I've already experienced, the life I've already lived.

I stare up at the ceiling, trying to think through who might want to hurt me, but I keep drawing a blank. Instead, I know I need to focus on saving myself; I'm not sure anyone else will.

I pull open my laptop, searching my database for the symbol Megan drew, the red craned arches, the same symbol that was on the handle of the knife allegedly found in my cabin, but I don't find anything. There are others, of course, images of brandings and logos for various organizations and cults that have popped up throughout the country over the last two decades, but nothing resembling the arches.

I close my laptop and push it into my backpack, making a mental note to look through the items in my home office. Maybe I can find something in a book or an interview that mentions the triple arch.

Locking up my office feels final. Keys in hand, I look to my left and then to my right down the hall, catching the eyes of coworkers. Maybe this morning I was imagining things when I thought people were watching me, judging me, but now I know for certain the truth is out. People know I'm not coming back to work. They know I've been accused of a crime.

Their looks warrant worry. I'm not judging them for that. This college isn't much different from anywhere else in the world. The rumor mill has begun to spin, and I'm not sure I want to know the story they're telling about me, the reclusive woman who kidnaps children.

God, it makes me wish I had social media so I could have posted about going to trivia night the other evening. At least then it would prove I'm not always alone, that I know how to be a social human being and make connections. But if I tried that now, it would look pathetic. Too little, too late.

I know where I need to go before I head back home. I walk to the law school building on campus and knock on Malcolm's door.

"One second," he calls out. "I'm just wrapping some things up."

I stand in the hallway, looking at my phone. There is an email from Charlotte.

Hey, Ms. Grace,

Sorry I won't be seeing you in class for a while, but I'm thinking about you.

Let me know if you need anything. We got your back!"

I don't even know how to reply to that. *Don't worry about me. I'm not actually a killer. I don't really kidnap children.* Anything I say will come across as defensive. I'm going to have to let the facts speak for themselves.

I should take heed of Holt's warning. Anything I do or say might be held against me, and that's the last thing I need. Before I reply to her or anyone else, I need the advice of a lawyer.

At that thought, Malcolm's door opens, and a student exits. "I'll see you later, Professor Balder," he says, before climbing the stairs at the end of the hallway.

"Hey," Malcolm smiles at me. "I wasn't expecting to see you today. What's up?" he asks. I follow him into his office. "That kid is hilarious. He's always reading about these obscure cases online, thinking he'll be able to solve them."

"Maybe he should be an FBI agent," I suggest with a smile.

"An FBI agent, huh? What do you know about them?"

"Actually," I reply, settling down into his comfy armchair, "more than I wish."

"Okay, now I'm curious. What's up?"

"So you haven't heard anything?"

"About what?" he asks. "Is there some good gossip?"

"Something like that," I groan. "God, it's been a hell of a few days since I saw you."

"Trivia day was literally two days ago."

"Exactly, and I've got to tell you what's happened since then."

I take some time explaining the situation. The motion detectors going off in the middle of the night. The little girl showing up at my door. The FBI agent coming a few hours later. Going to the station. The interviews, the interrogations, the warrant to search my cabin.

"Holy shit!" Malcolm exclaims. "This is shocking. All of this has happened, and you didn't call me?"

"Well, yesterday was a really long day. I was in an interview room for ages. I didn't realize I would show up to work today and be suspended."

"You were suspended? I'm surprised you weren't fired."

"Yeah, that's what the dean said too, that I should count my lucky stars. But Malcolm, I don't feel very lucky. I've been framed. Someone's trying to set me up, and I don't know why. I've never seen this kid before."

"The girl?"

"Yeah, Her name's Megan Talbot, although she doesn't really

refer to herself as that or anything. She won't speak. The girl's fragile. She's a total mess."

"I just don't understand how they thought you were involved in a kidnapping case that took place seven years ago."

"Someone planted evidence in my cabin. The murder weapon for one. Items the children owned were found in my home. I didn't put them there."

Malcolm looks at me. "You know, if you did, that would be one hell of a front. I would've never suspected it."

I look at him in shock. "Are you seriously trying to consider whether or not I'm guilty? God, nobody has faith in me."

"No, that's not what I'm suggesting at all," Malcolm explains.. "I'm just saying, wouldn't that be wild if you actually were this crazy lunatic fronting as a cult behavior specialist?"

"I'm not fronting anything," I deny, not enjoying Malcolm's joke. I know he's trying to make light of a hard situation, but it doesn't feel funny. It just feels grim.

"I'll do anything I can for you, I'll take on your case. Pro bono, of course."

"No, I'm not asking for any handouts."

"When Leon was struggling with depression a few years ago, you literally saved his life, Willow. I owe you so much. I'm eternally grateful for what you did for my son. You gave me my kid back."

"Yeah, well, the kid I just found, she went back to her mom this morning. I don't know if she's going to fare as well as Leon. She's really bad off. She wouldn't speak. She drew this symbol on a notepad, and I keep trying to find it in my database. I feel like someone has been keeping her hostage, keeping her captive for a long time. She's terrified of the police."

"You care about her?"

"Anyone would, she's a child."

Malcolm nods. "Look, if someone set you up, that's easy enough to prove. I don't know the ins and outs of all of this, details of the case, what they actually found searching your cabin, but I'll get on it right away."

"I have a camera system in my house," I tell him, desperate for some lead. "It should have shown any movement, but the officers seized that as well. That would've been the best way to prove my innocence. They could have seen when I was coming and going. Know that I didn't have any children, know that I didn't chase them through the woods. And who planted the things in my house."

"Look, I will work on the motion to get access to all the evidence that's against you, but I have to wait until you've been formally charged before I can make any legal motions."

"How long could that take?"

"I don't know, a day, two days? I'll call the sheriff's office to get a better idea. They usually want to be cooperative with lawyers."

"Not in this situation. They're hell-bent on proving me guilty."

"Then in the next few days, just lay low, stay off the radar."

"Well, that's what I've been doing for the better part of the last decade and look where it got me."

"Don't freak out, Willow. It's going to be okay. Do you want me to come over tonight? I could bring over some dinner."

“Thanks, but no, I'm just going to try to go home and clear my head. I haven't slept well. I've just been tossing and turning. I'm a mess, Malcolm. I don't want to lose everything for something I never even did."

"Listen, I'm going to reach out to the sheriff's office and let them know I'll be representing you from here on out. I'll find out the status of the arrest warrant and try to make the process as painless as possible for you. All right?"

"Thank you" Part of me wants to give him a hug. But that feels like an intimacy I can’t handle, especially after everything I have just been through. I look up at him, remembering our past. A year after I got hired here, Malcolm and I skirted the line of decency. He was interested in a relationship, I was in no place for that. I still am not.

"Thank you," I say again.

I leave the building and get in my car. As I drive away, I look in the rearview mirror, tears pricking my eyes, feeling more melancholy than I imagined I would.

I'm leaving the campus I've grown to love, and as it fades in the distance, I am forced to look ahead, with no idea of how I'm going to get myself out of this mess.

28 WILLOW GRACE

By the time I'm rounding onto my driveway, I have repeated the mantra my therapist taught me years ago. Repeated it enough times that my breathing has slowed, and I've calmed down.

I'm okay. I'm okay. What's happening in this moment will not be forever. I'm okay. I'm okay.

When you say things enough, a part of your brain makes them your new truth. That's what happens when people are brought into cults, into factions of people where your belief system is changed and conditioned.

It's not all that different from therapy.

Of course, therapy is not coercive. The patient handles their progress, not the other way around. Still, I hope I'm being conditioned for something better. *I'm okay. I'm okay.*

When I get to the end of the driveway in front of my cabin, I see two patrol cars parked in front of me. I veer to the right, parking out of the way, and then climb out of my car to see Deputy Howie and another officer exit their vehicles and approach me.

As I walk toward them, I get an alert on my phone. It's been delayed because of the intermittent cell signal, I assume. At first, I'm guessing it's a text message, but I see it's an alert from my camera system telling me that it's been dismantled and to call a 1-800 number for service help.

I'm not able to call the service number now to tell them the reason it's not operating is because it was confiscated by the sheriff's department, so I slide my phone in my pocket and call out in greeting, "What can I do for you guys?"

" I'm Deputy Howie. We've met, and this is Deputy Cruz."

"Well, Grace, we're here because we have a warrant for your arrest," Deputy Cruz announces.

I look at her. She's younger than me with a confidence I've never had, even when I'm in front of a class, well, with a class on a trail. I don't have the same sort of poise as she does. Her back is straight, her eyes are sharp, she's in control.

When I am in control, there is a layer of falsity, like I'm wearing a mask and putting on a brave face, because deep inside, I still have wounds that have not healed. Cruz, though, is all confidence.

I envy her, but my gaze shifts from her to Howie, who is reading me my Miranda Rights. "Anything you do or say can be held against you in a court of law."

"Can I go inside and get some things? I mean..."

"I'm sorry." Cruz says, "Right now, the only thing we're allowed to do is put you in custody."

"It's all a big mistake. Can I call my lawyer?"

"Eventually, yes."

I look at my cabin the same way I looked at the college just twenty minutes ago, as if it was something fading from my past, and my stomach rolls thinking that this place I've made into my private sanctuary might not be a part of my future.

They open the cruiser door and tell me to get in the back. I exhale, letting them lead me where I'm supposed to go, not wanting to put up a fight. But a small part of me wishes I would fight back somehow, run away, run free, just like Kevin and Megan must have done that night in the woods.

They didn't want to be caught, and neither do I. With a sinking realization, I know it's too late. I'm in the back of a police cruiser, headed to the station, charged with murder.

There's no time left to run. I'm already caught.

29 PAXTON HOLT

Back at my office the next day, I'm clearing the paperwork from the case. I look over some of my notes, not that they're extensive because everything that took place in Thurston County wrapped up so damn fast. So fast, in fact, it makes me sure that Willow is not responsible for what happened with Megan and Kevin. The sheriff and the deputies were so quick to make a move that it's impossible for me to believe they didn't make a mistake somewhere along the line.

When I review the notes about the evidence collected, I kick myself for not checking, or at least asking to see the locked room. It was a rookie mistake, just like I made seven years ago, not tracking down the people who took the kids. But I was right there in Willow's cabin; my hand was on the padlock. I asked her about it. She told me it went to the basement.

In that moment, I wish I would've been more aggressive, more direct and asked her to show me. It could have saved her and the sheriff's department so much time. And even if it hadn't, at least I would know for sure what was there to find. I could have asked Willow face-to-face with Megan there. It would've cracked things open in a whole different way. Instead, I wasn't there when the search warrant was put in. When they brought in evidence, I was with Megan in an interrogation room trying to find out the truth. Now it's been decided that Willow is to blame for everything.

My boss enters and I drop the notes I'm holding on my desk, feeling frustrated.

"What is it?" Tamara asks.

"I'm just feeling like I missed something. I should have done more to get Willow cleared before they took her into custody."

"Stop beating yourself up for things you don't need to. There's no need for a hero complex. You're not anybody's savior. You're an FBI agent, and you did your job. In fact, you did your job very well. That's why I came over here. I wanted to let you know I am putting your name in for an award."

"No, no, no," I shake my head. "I don't want any notoriety."

"I don't care, Holt. What you did was incredible. You found Megan."

"It doesn't feel incredible,We still don't know why her brother was murdered."

"Okay, can we separate the two? Megan's been missing for seven years. She's now reunited with her mother. That's a win, Paxton. Take it."

"I just feel like getting an award for finding her undermines the fact that I didn't find the kids in time to save her older brother."

"I understand it's complicated, but this job is hard, Paxton. You know that; you've been doing it for seven years. But when there is a win, when there is a W to claim, you got to hold on to it. Hell, and not just with the job. That's with life too, you know? If you have an opportunity to celebrate, celebrate. There's going to be enough hard shit getting in the way of that."

I look at her, her poise and her strength. She's got to be a fantastic mom.

"What?" she asks. "Now you're looking at me weird."

"I'm not. I'm just, I'm lucky to have a boss like you."

"Okay," she laughs. "I'll take that." She grins, pointing a finger at me. "See, you got to celebrate the victories. This kid agent over here thinks I'm the shit."

"Well, I didn't say that," I joke.

"Sure, but you were thinking it," she grins at me. "Anyway, you were just telling me how you wanted to move up in this department. Let me help you. An award like this, some recognition from other field offices, that'll do you good."

"Thanks.And not to beat a dead horse, but I really feel like something just doesn't fit. It's the why factor. Why would Willow do this? You haven't met her. You don't understand. She's not a killer."

Tamara's eyes rise. She leans against the cubicle. "Oh, wait, was there something that happened between you and Willow? Something I don't know about?"

"Nothing happened.I bought her a cheeseburger. I'm just saying I know people. I know bad people, and I know good ones. Willow is a good one."

"She's also someone who has a motive, Holt. She was filling a void. She was a woman with a mysterious past and intimately knows what goes through the minds of many criminals. There was evidence in her house. She's been living an isolated life and not involving the people from her work in it at all. She has no friends, no family. That's a lot of reasons to believe she could have done something unhinged. You got to let the facts lead you, not your heart."

"But what about intuition?" I ask her. "Doesn't that play a role in any of this?"

"To some degree, sure. But, Holt, it's not your case anymore. It's Thurston County's. Again, I'm going to leave you on a positive note. You're going to get an award, and you deserve it," she emphasizes, her voice firm as if wanting to prove something to me.

She walks away and my buddy Jedd looks over the cubicle. "What was that all about? You're buying some girl cheeseburgers?"

"Shut up!And it's not a girl. She's a professor."

"Ooh, fancy."

I roll my eyes and look back at my computer as my phone buzzes. It's a number I don't recognize, but I pick it up.

"Hi, this is Lucy, Megan's social worker."

"Hey," I say. "Is everything all right?"

"No, it's not. I'm trying to not freak out, but-"

"What?" I'm already standing, reaching for my keys. "What happened?"

"Megan's missing," she says. "I think she ran away from home. She's not here. No one knows where she is."

"What about her mom? What did Valerie say happened?"

"That's the problem. She's at the hospital. She was brought in this morning because of an overdose."

Dammit. I knew something wasn't right. "I'm on my way." I may not have saved Kevin, but I sure as hell am going to save Megan.

Maybe it is a hero complex, maybe I do want to be the savior.

But if it means Megan comes back home in one piece, breathing, living, fully alive, then I don't care what it makes me.

I think what it really makes me is a good fucking agent.

30 WILLOW GRACE

I'm in a small, dark room with only a sliver of light peeking under the doorway. I have a mattress on the ground, but nothing else. My feet are bare. I'm wearing a long cotton dress. The only jewelry I'm wearing is the simple golden band on my ring finger.

I twist it around out of habit.

If I twist it enough, I wonder if the metal will wear away until it's gone.

As I lay there in the dark, I try not to panic. I try to count. How many hours has it been? How many days? Too many. I try not to cry. I try not to tremble. It's impossible though. This is my life.

Paying penance for things I have done wrong, choices I've made that were not approved of.

Talking too loudly, laughing too much, walking from one corridor to the next without asking permission from my husband. It's all I know, this life, and it's a small one.

I blink, tossing and turning on the mattress in the jail cell. The memory that has surfaced has been a part of my life for so long.

The fact I got a second chance from that existence feels like a miracle.

But now my new reality hits hard. I've been charged for kidnapping and murder. This new life of mine feels like a sick joke.

I worked so hard to escape that life of confinement, of rules, and of brainwashing. It's why I worked so hard with my education, why I made it a point to give back, to help other people escape. But now, as I look across the jail cell, I'm just as trapped as ever.

When I got here yesterday, I was booked and processed, things I had only ever seen in movies, nothing I thought would ever actually happen to me.

They recorded my name and the crime I was charged with. I had a surreal moment when they took my mug shot, capturing my mental and physical condition forever. I can only imagine how hollow I looked in that image, the flash blinding me for a moment, none of it feeling real.

They took my fingerprints one after the other, which is something I've always feared. I don't want to be in a system.

I don't want to be identified by anyone. But now I'm in a database and can be identified if I'm a perpetrator of any other crime in the future. But that wasn't the worst. The worst was the full body search. A deeply humiliating moment, a strip search to make sure that I wasn't bringing any weapons or drugs into the jail.

The booking officers required me to remove all my clothing and submit to a full body search. The whole time, I wondered who was requesting this. It wasn't necessary. But the officer who performed it told me a strip search is legal, especially when brought in for such a large crime.

I told her I wasn't arrested for something dangerous.

She looked at me like I was crazy. "You've been charged with murder."

The word sent a chill over me. Another reality of just how bad things were. The booking officer told me they were checking if I had any other warrants for my arrest. I looked at her like she was off her rocker because that's how it felt.

I've never committed any criminal activity. I've only done my best to live a small, simple life. Now, I fear my life just got even smaller, even more simple because I'm in a cell.

A door opens at the end of the hall, and I see Sheriff Moon walking toward me, carrying a file folder. He looks in on me, glaring, and I want to yell at him, which isn't even in my typical wheelhouse. I'm not a yeller – I can stay calm under pressure. But this is an entirely new circumstance. This is my life.

I want to tell him this is wrong. This isn't fair, that someone else did this. Someone is out to get me. But I've been advised not to speak to anybody without the presence of my attorney.

Moon stands still, looking at me with a menacing gaze. "Looks like you've been holding back on who you really are. See, fingerprints don't lie and yours did not come back to your name, Willow Grace. I guess I should be calling you Lila Montgomery, right?"

I shudder. I haven't heard that name in a very long time, and I had hoped to never hear it again. I don't want to explain to him why I changed my name, why I had to.

Tears fill my eyes, and I blink them away, hating that I'm giving this man any part of myself. I want to keep it all back, save my emotion for a time when it matters. My hands turn to fists. I squeeze them tight. I lower my head, refusing to give him anything.

Moon clears his throat and asks, "You want to tell me where you were last night, after you left Conifer College, before you got home?"

I swallow, choosing my words with care. "I'd like to speak with my attorney."

"You'll speak with your attorney before the arraignment. Until then, you can sit and wallow in your lies, Lila," he scoffs.

I look at him as he walks away, wanting to know why Moon asked that question. I bite my bottom lip, wondering why it mattered to him.

The only thing I can think of is something's happened to Megan.

31 PAXTON HOLT

When I showed up at this complex yesterday morning to meet Megan's mom and be a part of the unification process, I was holding on with a thread of hope, hope that things would work out for this little girl. After all the hell she's been through, she deserves it.

I wouldn't say I had a ton of confidence in her mother's ability to parent her, but I also know that might be my jaded past catching up with me. I walked away, wanting to believe things would be okay. But coming back now, such a short time later, I realize the thread is gone. There's nothing to hold on to. It's lost, just like she is.

Uniformed patrolmen from the Seattle Police Department are scattered about, and I walk over to the most senior sergeant, Conrad, introducing myself.

"You were the one who found the girl. Is that right?" he asks me.

I nod. "Yes, just a few days ago. It's tragic that she's already on the run again, or worse," I venture, running a hand over my jaw.

"Well, we don't have any updates on her, unfortunately. but none of it looks good, though. Maybe someone who had taken her in the first place came back for her, or maybe she just got spooked and ran.

The mom got high. Maybe the girl got scared when she flatlined and took off. She'll probably turn up."

"When did you get the call?" I ask.

Conrad clears his throat. "The social worker came by early with donuts wanting to make sure the first night was a success. She found the door open. She entered the apartment and found the mother overdosed on the floor, a goddamn needle sticking out of her arm."

I shake my head. "Hadn't she been clean for 10 months?"

Conrad gives me a hard look, as if I'm an idiot, a look I feel like I've been getting all too often lately from the upper ups in the police departments I've been dealing with. "Once a junkie, always a junkie, right?"

It's hard to hear him say such a thing, even though in my experience, I'd say it's pretty damn true. But what I don't like about this is that these officers have already drawn their own conclusions about what happened to Megan.

"Can I look inside?" I ask. "Inside the apartment?"

Conrad shrugs. "I don't care. Detectives are en route, so you have permission to enter."

"Thanks," I say, knowing he is breaking protocol, but not questioning it.

Walking inside, I immediately notice the place is in disarray. It wasn't like this yesterday, when there was some order. How can so much go downhill so damn fast? Trash on the living room floor. What looks like a pot of macaroni and cheese is discarded on a stovetop. There's a box of cereal ripped open on the counter. Not that leaving a mess in the kitchen is a red flag, but when I look in the bedrooms, it reminds me of my own childhood, when my mom would get chaotic and lose control, when her episodes would take over reason.

There's a liquor bottle on the coffee table, a pack of cigarettes, and an ashtray full of stubs. In the bedroom, there's an empty bottle of tequila. I feel sick to my stomach thinking of that little girl being here last night. It's too much for anyone, especially a child.

In the bedroom, where I'm assuming Megan slept, I find her doll left behind. I pick it up thinking even when she left wherever she'd been held captive for seven years, she took this with her. Why would she leave it behind now?

I sit on the bed, holding it in my hand, and under the sheets, I feel a book. I pull it out. It's a spiral-bound notebook. Flipping it open, I see several drawings of the symbol that she made for me in the interrogation room two days ago.

One page after the other, three arches. I do see it sort of like a rainbow, but there's no happy lines of color, no cheerful clouds or sun. It's three sharp arches, every one of them in red.

I swallow, flipping the pages. The entire book is filled with that symbol. On the last page though, it's different.

I look at the drawing Megan made, and I see it's of a girl and a woman holding hands. There are trees all around them. The sky is blue. She didn't miss any details: birds chirping; sun in the sky; wildflowers growing up from the green grass.

At first, I assume it's a drawing of her and her mother, but the closer I look, I realize the details of the drawing resemble Willow and her cabin. The drawing shows a little cabin perched in the distance, and the girl and the woman walk toward it. A woman with a long brown braid and blue jeans.

That is not a picture of Megan's mom with her cropped blue hair. And in the picture, the two are holding hands. There's nothing harsh about the image. It's all soft. I wish I could pull it out of the notepad and tuck it into my pocket to give to Willow later, but I know I can't do such a thing.

Still, in my heart, it reinforces my belief that Willow could not have been responsible for such a heinous act. Megan wouldn't care this much for the woman if she killed her brother.

I take a quick photo of the drawing so I can show Willow later. Then I close the notepad, setting it on the bedside table, and placing the doll on top. As I pass through the front door, I noticed pry marks near the lock, like a crowbar went at it. I mentioned this to Conrad as I left.

"There's damage on the door," I say, as I exit the complex.

"Oh yeah? I didn't notice."

"I think someone should check it out, see how long the marks have been there."

"Well, this place is for junkies in recovery, so I wouldn't expect much different. I wouldn't doubt it if it's been there for years. People looking for drug money, you know?"

"Sure," I say, "but it could also be connected to this case."

"I'll check it out," he says. But the way he dismisses me doesn't give me any peace of mind.

As I'm about to walk out of the building, Conrad calls me back. "Agent Holt,thought you might like to know--"

"What?" I ask, turning to him.

"Just got word from the hospital. Megan's mother died."

I want to swear, but I don't.

Instead, I simply pull my card from my wallet and hand it to Conrad. "Call me the moment the girl is found."

32 WILLOW GRACE

I'VE BEEN SITTING in this interview room alone for the last ten minutes, watching the clock on the wall hanging over the door. It's hard not to overthink things, but the last twenty-four hours have felt like hell.

The way Sheriff Moon looked at me this morning when he passed my cell turned my blood cold. It didn't give me any confidence that I would get out of here anytime soon. But then I was brought into this interview room and told my lawyer would meet with me shortly, and relief filled my chest.

Malcolm knocks on the door, pushing it open. "Willow," he says in greeting.

I stand, walking toward him. I don't care if it's not professional or it crosses bounds, I wrap him in a hug.

He laughs. "Okay. Okay. You all right there?"

I pull away from him, squeezing his shoulders. "Thank you for coming. It's been hell," I reply, taking my seat again.

He sits opposite me, shaking his head. "I can only imagine."

I give him a bit of a snort, because what are you supposed to say to this? The entire situation is mind-numbingly insane. The fact that I am sitting here at all, being accused of a crime I didn't commit.

"Did everything go okay with getting booked and processed?" he asks. "I know that can be traumatic for some people."

"That's an understatement. The mug shot alone made me feel like I was being sentenced to something. It felt so final. The flash, you know?"

"I don't from personal experience," Malcolm answers.

"Right. Well, I hope you can keep it that way. None of it's been pleasant. That jail cell is so cold. It's like they want me to be miserable."

"I think they do," he says. "Especially you. You're their prime suspect. They want you to break."

"There's nothing for me to break. I didn't do anything. I'm not holding back a secret. I don't have some hidden agenda."

I look up at the camera in the corner. "Is that recording everything? Because if it is, I'm not going to talk. I just feel like I've said too much already."

"Don't worry," he assures me. "The recording device is off, and if I find out any of our discussion has been recorded or observed, heads will roll. Okay? You can trust me on that."

"Thank you," I say, taking a deep breath.

"Look, this is the case as it's laid out against you," he begins. "They found the weapon in your home. They found the children's personal items in your house. You had a security system that was keeping everyone away. You had an entire room dedicated to brainwashing practices. Megan is loyal to you. She trusts you, someone you're claiming you just met. Doesn't add up, Willow."

"I didn't kill Kevin Talbot," I'm incredulous. "I know it sounds terrible, but what do you think? I feel like I'm wracking my brain for an answer that isn't going to be found. Who has it out for me?"

"Maybe it's not about you. Maybe it's about pinning it on you to protect someone else."

I nod. "I mean, that makes more sense. What do you think is going to happen?"

"Honestly, it all looks pretty bad, Willow. We need a piece of evidence to refute the claim. That's all. If we can prove that someone planted the weapon in your house, then you're free. At least as good as free. But look, I have some questions."

"Okay. But I've told you everything about that night, about that morning."

"Not about that. It's about your name change and the fact your prints were on file from a time when you were arrested for stealing."

I press my hands to my temples. "Christ. I was eighteen. I had just left." I pause. "I had just left home and was hungry. I went to a Walmart, and I stole a loaf of bread and a jar of peanut butter, and I got caught and yeah, that looks bad."

"In that report, your name was Lila Montgomery."

"Right," I say. "It was right after I had escaped."

"Escaped?" he repeats.

I exhale. "Yeah. After I left home, it was a bad situation, and I wanted to turn my life around. That's why I got my name changed, and I left the past behind. I got into college and became a different person."

"But you see how that looks bad, right?"

"I guess," I say. "I didn't even remember my prints would be on file, because it was under a different name. I'm such an idiot." I shake my head.

"Why did you need to run from your past?"

"The people in my life before were dangerous." I shake my head, not wanting to say anymore, hating parts of my story.

"How dangerous? Like if the police knew, they'd be involved, dangerous?"

I press my lips together, not wanting to answer. This is my secret, and it's what has kept me alive all these years. I'm not going to reveal it now, not in the middle of this investigation.

"Look, that's not all, we have more problems than that."

"Like what?" I ask. Looking around the small interview room, I wish like hell I could just get outside for ten minutes to take in a deep breath and breathe. I hate being stuck in here. I feel myself tensing, my foot tapping, my body shaking..

"You okay?" Malcolm asks.

"It's just a lot," I murmur. "And you said there's more. It's overwhelming."

"Look, I need to know where you were last night. Yesterday, when you..."

"Where was I? Yesterday? I went to work and then my class was canceled. I got called into the dean's office, and that's when I went and talked to you."

"What did you do after that?"

"I went back to my office. I was there for several hours, just packing my stuff, trying to process it all."

"All right."

"And then after I packed up my stuff, I drove home. That's when I saw the patrol cars and was brought in."

"Did you stop anywhere else?"

"Why?"

"I need you to answer the question first."

"I was ready to get home. I was exhausted. But I drove to Tacoma for dinner. I stopped at that taqueria on the corner of 4th and Prospect, and I got food. I was probably in there twenty-five, thirty minutes."

"Why did you go to Tacoma?"

"I knew this taqueria had great street tacos, and I had a really shit day, and I was feeling sorry for myself, and I thought chips and guacamole and a margarita might help."

"You know where that taco shop is located?" he asks, pulling out his phone on Google Maps. He turns it to me. "It's about two miles from where Megan and her mom are."

"They're in Tacoma?" I ask. "I thought they were from Seattle."

"That's where they were taken seven years ago. But her mom now lives in Tacoma, which is about what, twenty minutes from you?" he says.

"I had no idea that's where they were living. And how could I? I don't even know her mom's name."

"Right. But imagine the court. Imagine what they would think, because if the case against you is that you are the one who took her seven years ago, they would believe you were keeping tabs on the mom all that time."

"But I wasn't. I just wanted a taco."

"Sure. But saying you went straight home, when in fact, you were a few miles from where Megan was... Look, I'm not saying you're guilty..."

"But you're not saying I'm innocent. So what? Now, you're doubting me too?"

"I didn't say that."

I shake my head frustrated. "Why does it even matter if I was a few miles from where Megan happened to be? What difference does it make? Megan's with her mom now, I am in jail. I'm completely unconnected to the whole thing."

"Except there's more. Remember I wanted to tell you about something?"

"Right. Sorry, what is it?"

"Megan's mother overdosed in the early hours of this morning. She's dead. And no one has seen Megan since yesterday."

My breath catches, and Malcolm continues speaking.

"The social worker went this morning to check on them and found the mother with a needle in her arm and the girl gone."

"Oh my God," I say, pressing my fingers to my temples. "I need to speak with Special Agent Holt immediately."

"I'll see what I can do," Malcolm tells me.

"Did you have a chance to review the video footage from my cabin? That is the only thing I can imagine that would be able to prove my innocence. It could show who came and who went."

"I'm sorry, Willow. I really didn't want to bring this up, but the recordings were completely corrupted and wiped out. Sheriff Moon and his team are having it sent to the state right now for digital forensics at the lab to see if they can salvage any of the footage, but it's not looking good."

"Dammit," I suddenly remember there is backup footage on my phone. "Then I need access to my cell phone. That would help me prove who could have set me up."

"On your phone?"

"Yes, there's backup data there from my security system. Maybe that can help."

Malcolm seems rejuvenated by this idea. "I'll see what I can do. We'll do anything we can to help you, Willow."

"Thank you, for all of this. I know you're busy. You don't even take on cases anymore. The fact you're doing this at all. You're a good friend."

"Well, we all care about you, Willow." His eyes meet mine, saying more than his words do.

"Thanks," I tell him again, not wanting to lead him on, but also needing his help.

As he's gathering his things to leave, Deputy Howie arrives at the door. He pokes his head in. "Hey, Willow. I wanted to let you know Holt is here. He wanted a chance to speak with you."

Malcolm looks over at me. I nod. Malcolm clears his throat. "Great. Send him in."

33 WILLOW GRACE

Deputy Sheriff Howie leaves to get Special Agent Holt. I look at Malcolm. "Look, I want to speak with Holt, but I was wondering if I could speak with him alone."

Malcolm gives me a hard look. "That's not exactly orthodox," he hesitates.

"I realize that. I just want a moment alone with him."

He nods slowly. "Is there something I should know about?"

"No, I promise."

He gives me a tight nod. "Then I'm going to go follow up on some of these things, all right?"

"Thank you."

"Look," Malcolm assures me, "I will do my best to help you, but I suggest you do your best to help yourself."

He leaves, and a few minutes later, Holt comes in. It's not that I wanted to hurt Malcolm's feelings, but I feel comfortable with Holt in a way I don't feel with anyone else.

All that changes the moment he walks into the room because his eyes are hard. His mouth is set in a firm line, and even though he has chiseled features and strong shoulders, right now it's not strength I see, it's anger.

"Megan's missing," he states.

"I heard," I admit.

"Yeah? What did you do, Willow? What did you do here?"

"What did I do? I've been in jail since yesterday evening. The girl went missing this morning. What do you think I did?"

Clearly pissed, he grumbles, "Twenty-four hours and the girl's gone again." He shakes his head, pacing the small room, making it feel smaller than I already find it.

I take a deep breath in and out. *I'm okay, I'm okay*. But am I?

I swallow. "Listen, Holt, I couldn't have kidnapped her, okay? And I'm not working with anybody who did it on my behalf. I didn't kill her mother. It sounds like she killed herself."

"Something's off," he almost shouts. "Dammit!" He slams his fist on the table.

I startle, pulling back, surprised to see this side of him, the passion. "You care about her."

"Of course I care about her. I failed her seven years ago, Willow. Because of my failure, her brother died."

"I didn't do it."

"I know you didn't do it, but something is off about this case. And I was hoping when I came in here you could give me some sort of answer, but now I'm realizing, how could you? You have been in here the last twenty-four hours. You have nothing to do with this, but somebody does."

"I know," I say, "and until we know who, it's pretty difficult to get me out of here."

"Is there anything you think could help the situation? Help get Megan back?"

"I asked Malcolm to check on a few things. Apparently my security system at the house was completely wiped out, and I don't know who did that or why, but I guess Sheriff Moon is trying to get it all recovered."

"Okay," Holt says, nodding, tracking with me.

"My phone has backup data of everything that was on that camera. It has all the footage of who might have come and gone over the last week. Someone wiped out my security system data, but they didn't know the backup footage was accessible. I need my phone."

"All right. Give me a minute."

I'm surprised by how quickly he walks out of the room. He didn't even press me for more information about what may or may not be on my phone. He simply listened, took it in, and believed me. I appreciate his ability to take control of a situation, not like men I've known before who take control in order to hurt. He took control in order to help.

I sit back in the chair feeling more at ease than I have since I first entered the sheriff's department, feeling like Holt is on my side, and that alone is a gift I wasn't expecting. For all outward appearances, he should be the last person I trust, a man in authority with power, money, and prestige. But that's not how I feel when I'm around him. I feel like, if there are sides in this world, good and bad, he's on the side I want to be on.

When he returns several minutes later, he is holding my phone. I exhale. The relief I feel seeing that device alone is shocking.

"You got it."

"Hey, sometimes being charming helps."

I laugh, despite myself, turning on the phone and pulling up the app I use for the backup to the camera system.

Holt pulls a chair around the table sitting next to me.

"Look," I say, "You can see me and Megan on the porch. That's the day she knocked on the door. You can see her coming up on the porch steps, then me opening the door and talking to her and bringing her inside."

"I see that," Holt says, "but that doesn't exactly prove your innocence. Maybe she was out in the middle of the night."

I frown, scrolling back to where Holt arrived at my house. "Look, see, you came here now. And then look." I keep scrolling closer to before the search warrant would've happened. "This is when Moon arrived; he's standing outside on my porch on the phone."

"I wish the audio worked," Holt says.

"I know, it doesn't come through. I've always had trouble with that. It works better on the main panel in the house. Okay, so Moon arrived to prepare for the search."

"We knew that. Everything looks good, Willow, this isn't proving anything."

"But look. No, look, look!" I'm speeding it up now. About ten minutes later, another vehicle arrives in a beat-up pickup truck. There's no front plate on it, which means Holt can't track it.

A young man exits the vehicle. He's carrying a duffle bag over his shoulder. Sheriff Moon greets the man, and, again, I'm wishing I had audio.

They talk for a minute or two on the porch before they both enter the cabin. Several minutes later, they exit as a pair. "What were they doing in there?" Holt asks, as we watch them have another brief exchange on the porch and a handshake. Then the unknown young man gets back into his truck and drives away.

At that point, though, I'm able to freeze frame the departing truck and zoom in enough to get a license plate. My heart is racing with hope.

"Give me a sec," he says, "I'm going to go run this." He gives me a hard look before he walks away and adds, "Willow, I think it's going to be okay. This is what we needed."

"Thank God," I say, relief flooding my body.

A few minutes later, Agent Holt and Malcolm enter the interview room. They have satisfied looks on their faces.

"What is it?" I ask. "Tell me something good, please."

"We ran the plates," Holt says, "We found that they belong to an Earl Dawson. And his last known address isn't far from where you live, five miles maybe."

"Okay, so you can go find him?"

"Yes, and whatever doubt regarding your innocence has been

completely removed. This information alone means the charges are going to be dropped."

"Really?" I ask. "Just like that?"

"Sheriff Moon has been lying and planting evidence."

"I guess your gut was right," I say to Holt. "You knew something was wrong."

"Of course, I know you aren't t a killer, Willow Grace."

Agent Holt tells Malcolm to get this phoned to the prosecution and have the charges dropped.

"I'm on it," Malcolm says.

"But after you do that," Holt adds, "you need to come right back to this room, and you're not to leave Willow's side. No matter what."

34 MEGAN TALBOT

KEVIN WAS the one who wanted to leave Harmony. At first, when he started mentioning it, I didn't understand why. I thought this was our home, our family, our mom and dad.

He was trying to explain it so I could understand, but it's hard because he remembers things I don't.

I was so little when we came here. The flashes I have of a life before Harmony almost seem like make believe. I remember being at a park and playing in the sand, and Kevin was on a swing, and he was swinging so high, it's like he could touch the sky.

I remember gasping because it looked like he was going to fly away, just like the birds. And I know that memory isn't from Harmony, because we don't have a sandbox there. We don't have a swing set. So how would I even know what that is unless I had some sort of memory from before?

I've told Kevin about that memory of the park, and he tells me it was a great day, one of his favorite days. He told me we had a picnic, and that day mom was happy and she had cut our sandwiches into little triangles. Mine was cheese and his was peanut butter and jelly, and we were fitting them together like a puzzle.

We whispered about this in the middle of the night when he came into my room at Harmony to make sure I was okay after one of my penances. I had been carrying rocks up a hill for hours. Father Benjamin had said it was to make me strong, to make me brave. I want to be strong and brave, but I didn't like the way my muscles hurt after I did that work for the entire day. My hands were bleeding. My heart, it felt like it was bleeding too.

When Kevin came into my room and told me to think about something happy, to forget about the day I just had and imagine the best day ever, a good memory, that's the one I told him.

He said I had only been three years old that day, but good memories always run deep inside of us. We can always hold them tight, and we can always remember them when we need them most.

I need them most right now, because I am lost, and I am scared. I didn't like Harmony, the only home I remember knowing, but this is worse.

At least at Harmony there was green grass and gigantic trees with trunks so wide I couldn't wrap my arms around them. And there was always good food. There I had my friends and my brother. At Harmony my brother was alive, and now he is gone. And I'm in a city I don't know, and I'm in an alley I've never seen.

I don't like this feeling.

It's raining, and I'm not wearing a coat. The rain has soaked through my shoes. I'm not wearing socks, and I'm hungry.

A few days ago, I lost my brother. This morning I lost my mom, and I didn't even know her.

And now she's gone before I had a chance to find out what she was like. I don't know why Earl did what he did. I was hiding in the bedroom, peeking out the door when he entered, jamming a crowbar into the door and forcing his way in.

Mom was screaming. She was terrified. We had been having a good day. We had made macaroni and cheese from a box, which is something I've never had before. And she got root beer, another new thing. We played a game of Clue in the living room while we ate, and I won with the candlestick in the ballroom with Professor Plum.

I went to bed thinking things might actually be okay. I don't know this lady who's my mom, but she seemed like she was doing her best to take good care of me. And she seemed so happy I was there, and I wanted her to be happy. Alone in my room, though, at night, I kept remembering Harmony. I was drawing it in my sketchbook, which Mom bought me, which I thought was awfully nice.

Even though I know she's my mother, she seems like a stranger. And I feel like she might be on edge, like any minute something could snap. I don't like that feeling. That's the feeling I always had at Harmony with Father Benjamin. Like if I did just the wrong thing and someone noticed, I'd be paying penance. I hate paying penance.

I wipe my eyes, leaning against the brick wall in the alley, wrapping my arms around my knees, trying not to tremble, trying not to shake, but it's too hard. I let myself cry.

The picture I drew wasn't of this lady who's my new mom, and it wasn't of Harmony. It was of me and Willow Grace, the nicest person I've ever met. And I know that might be weird to say about a lady I just met, but when she looked at me, I felt safe. When she made a bath for me, I felt warm, and when she combed my hair, I felt like I was home. I've never felt like I've been home before.

I don't know why Earl came into the apartment. It was so early; it woke me up. I jumped out of bed and poked my head through the bedroom door, and I saw him there. He grinned at me.

Earl is a terrible person. He killed my brother, and he's always hated us both. I think he's scared because he wants to be important to Father Benjamin. But the only reason Benjamin keeps him around is because he's strong, and strong people are always the ones in charge.

I looked at Earl, and he told me to shut up and stay put. So I didn't leave the bedroom, but I kept the door open a crack, and I watched what he did. He pushed my mom to the floor, and he pulled things out of his coat that scared me.

The needle was the scariest.

I closed my eyes because I didn't want to see. And even though I'd never been around something like that, I knew it was bad when he forced her to the ground, pressing his hand over her mouth. She kicked him. She bit him. He called her ugly names.

Tears streaked down my cheeks the whole time. He opened a big, black duffel bag and started putting things all around the house like bottles of alcohol. He was messing things up, making it look worse than it was. All she did with me was play a game and eat macaroni and cheese and do her best.

I knew Earl was going to come for me next, and I didn't want to go with him. I tiptoed to the bedroom window, opening it up, looking to see how far down I'd have to go. Three flights, but there was a stairwell. As quietly as I could, I left.

Earl isn't like Kevin. Kevin would've been smart enough to know this was an option, that I could have run away before he got to me. But Earl is just strong. He doesn't have the brains to back it up.

He's not someone I should be scared of, but I am now, alone in the alley. I'm not sure what's going to happen. I can't stay here for long. The rain is coming down, and I'm cold. I wish I was at Willow Grace's cabin with a fireplace roaring and pancakes on a plate.

A big white van pulls down the alley with its lights on. I panic because it's not slowing down. Earl is driving.

I stand and run, scared. He jumps out of the van. "You little bitch," he says. "You're not getting away this time!"

And even though I try, my foot catches on a rock, and I fall. My hands bleed the same way they did when I was carrying rocks up the hill for my penance. He lunges for me, wrapping me up in his arms and tossing me in the van, telling me to shut up if I know what's good for me.

If I know what's good for me? Does that even matter anymore?

I know what's good for me. It's being far away from him.

I wish I could sleep to block this out, forget it all. Earl uses a roll of duct tape to cover my mouth, then bind my hands behind my back. I cry silent tears, wishing I was stronger, capable of overtaking him.

Soon he's driving, muttering under his breath about Father Benjamin, about me getting what's due, about how he's proving himself to Father by getting me back. It's the only way he can prove his worthiness.

He's spiraling, even I can see that.

"Did you kill her?" I ask him through the tape, my words muffled, lost. "Did you kill my mother?"

He glares back at me. "Shut up. Sit down." For a moment I think maybe I'll just swing open the door and roll out. But the door is locked.

"Where are we going?" I try to ask, but it's impossible to speak through the tape covering my mouth.

"I told you to shut up unless you want to end up dead."

But I know he's not going to kill me, because he wasn't supposed to kill Kevin. Father Benjamin wants me back. I know I'm going back to Harmony in one piece.

Problem is, I don't want to go back there at all.

35 PAXTON HOLT

THE MOMENT I step out of the interview room where I had been with Willow and her lawyer, I let my shoulders fall, exhaling in relief. Willow isn't a killer. It's not that I've known this woman very long or very closely, but there is something about her that's very unique. I'm drawn to it. Her subtle way of looking at the world without an edge of bitterness. I didn't want to imagine a woman like her could be a killer. And she's not.

I pull out my phone and call the Seattle field office making sure my buddy Jedd knows what's going on.

"Hey," I say. "I need you to run some plates."

"I'm on it," he says, without any questions.

That's what makes me trust him. Trust the agents in general. They don't need extra details when it comes to taking care of the crimes we're tasked with solving.

"Are you still at the jail in Thurston County?" he asks me.

"Yeah," I answer, not wanting to get into it.

"And why aren't you asking those guys to run the plates?" he asks.

"Honestly, I don't trust them."

"Shit," Jedd whistles. "That sounds like a bad situation."

"It is," I say, thinking that's an understatement.

"Okay, I'll send you the information as soon as I have it," he tells me.

"Great, I'm going to call Tamara."

I end the call with Jedd and call my boss. My supervisor is surprised to hear me, to hear that I'm back in Thurston County. I had to come back, and God, am I glad I did.

"What's going on?" she asks.

I fill her in on the ever-evolving case. The situation with Sheriff Moon and how he was a part of planting the evidence in Willow's cabin.

"She had it all on her phone," I explain. "The data was backed up from her security system, and even though the sheriff's department must have wiped her surveillance cameras clean when they did the search warrant, they didn't access this."

"Wow," Tamara says. "I'm shocked, but I probably shouldn't be. Here's my question though. Why does Sheriff Moon w ant to plant this evidence on Willow?"

"Exactly!, I've been wanting to know the same thing. I need to get someone on Moon immediately and make sure he doesn't go anywhere. Until we follow him and see what he's up to, we're not going to know what his motive is."

I catch movement from the other side of the jail. "Oh shit!" I exclaim.

"What is it?" Tamara asks.

"He's on the move. Moon is leaving the sheriff's office right now. I'm going to follow him."

"All right. But I'm going to send some backup."

"Good.Can you track my location?"

"Yep, we got you," she tells me.

"I'm going to start following him. Okay?"

"I'm going to stay on the phone with you," Tamara decides. "Wouldn't want you to do anything stupid."

I chuckle, turning on the engine. My phone tethers immediately to the Bluetooth system in my car.

"You still there?" she asks.

"I'm here."

"Listen," she warns me. "Keep your distance and wait until we get a lock on the suspect vehicle."

I know she means well. She wants to keep me safe as an agent and as a friend, but I've got to follow Moon right now. I can't lose him.

If I do, I might never know why he was pinning the kidnapping of Megan and the death of her brother Kevin on Willow Grace.

36 WILLOW GRACE

THERE IS a sharp pang of relief when Holt leaves the interview room to run the plates on whoever that man was at my cabin with Sheriff Moon. I know I've been wrongly accused, and the fact that I was able — on my own — to prove my innocence gives me a sense of strength I've been missing for a long time. It's incredible the way validation can boost your confidence.

"I'm going to go arrange to have your charges dropped," Malcolm tells me.

I exhale. "Thank you."

"I'll be back. All right?"

"Thank you," I repeat.

Alone in the interview room I look up at the camera, thinking about all the ways we are watched, observed, and scrutinized in this life by so many people with so many motives. I still don't understand what Sheriff Moon's motive was. It's like he was watching me and making a calculated decision based on what he knew of my life, which, in reality, was not much.

Still, he knew he could pin, or at least attempt to pin, Megan's kidnapping and Kevin's death on me.

The question is why? Why would a man like him be involved in this kidnapping and murder in the first place? Until I know, I won't be able to rest or find peace. Added to that layer of heaviness is the reality that Megan is missing again.

Her mother died the first night they were reunited, and now she's alone in this world, a ten-year-old-girl running the streets of Tacoma. It's terrifying.

I remember to take my deep breaths in and out as I wait for Malcolm to return. My mind is spinning thinking about Megan and the arched symbol she drew. I feel like I've seen it before, that it's been brought up in some part of my research. I just can't seem to place it.

When Malcolm enters the interview room again, he's smiling. "Well, I arranged to have your charges dropped. But the evidence in question is being held by the prosecution with instructions not to release anything to the sheriff's office."

"My phone included?" I ask.

He nods. "Yeah. I'm sorry about that. But it's essential to this discovery, that data on your phone. It was the closest thing I've ever seen to guilt. I just don't understand why he is helping whoever that young man is."

"What does Sheriff Moon want by pinning this on me?"

"To get away with murder. Plain and simple. Let's go get your things."

Soon I'm changed back into my own clothes with my purse in hand; the only thing I don't have is my phone. We see Deputy Howie in the hall as we're getting ready to go.

"I could give you a lift home if you'd like," he offers.

I look over at Malcolm and shake my head. "Thanks, but no thanks."

Howie frowns. "Do you want to explain what's going on?"

"No," I reply. "Not to you."

His eyes widen, and he looks over at Malcolm. "What's this about?"

"I don't think I'm going to be talking to anybody at this sheriff's department anytime soon."

He frowns but lifts his hands in defense. "All right," he says. "I'm not going to press you."

"Good," I just walk away with Malcolm.

It's cold outside, but the rain has stopped and for that I am grateful. It still feels cooler than most Septembers here in Washington. Like a chill has set in over the week with everything that's transpired.

On the drive home Malcolm tries to make small talk. "Plans for the weekend? Excited to get back to school?"

I mumble one-word answers because I don't have the capacity to engage right now. Not when so much is still on my mind.

"I'm sorry. I'm just distracted."

"What are you distracted by specifically?"

I laugh. "Do you really have to ask?"

"Well, you're no longer involved in the situation with Sheriff Moon."

"I know," I say. "But he wanted to pin murder on me."

"I get that. I just wonder if it's about something else. Something more."

I swallow, looking out the window as we drive toward my cabin, down my gravel driveway. Home in the distance. "I'm just scared for that little girl. There's something about her I connected with. I want her to be safe. I want the best for her."

He nods. "You realize, Willow, you might never even see her again."

"I know that," I say defensively. "But it doesn't mean she's not on my mind."

He parks his car in front of my house, and we both get out. He lingers. "I want to make sure the house is secure. That you're not in any danger out here all alone."

"You're worried about me?" I ask.

"Of course I am. I've always worried about you."

I give him a wry smile. "Yeah, well, you shouldn't."

He shakes his head. "You don't always have to be so tough, you know."

"I'm not being tough. I'm being honest. You don't need to worry about me."

I unlock the front door of my house, and we both step inside. I feel uncomfortable at first, thinking of him being inside my home. I have always felt so protective of my space, and after the search, I feel that more strongly than ever.

But then he speaks, "Are you okay with me coming inside? I don't want you to feel like you have to let me in."

I exhale, remembering that he is looking out for me. That he is someone I can trust. "Thanks for saying that, but you can come in. I was able to put some things back in order before they hauled me to the station. But it still looks like it's been rifled through."

"They really weren't messing around when they searched your place, huh?"

"No,Is it always this aggressive?"

"I'm not sure, but they seriously did a number on your cabin."

"I know."

He walks around inspecting things, but I know where I need to be. I pull open the door of the small room that's usually padlocked. I step inside.

So much of it is disheveled and ripped apart, but I know what I'm looking for. I dig through files and old notebooks, flipping through pages one after the other. I remember a client from a few years ago who had been a member of a cult somewhere in Washington state.She needed help to process some of the trauma she had endured at this place. I remember the name. It was called The Harmony, and I swear the symbol is similar. I just need to see it now to make sure I've not lost my mind.

Remembering her name was Becky Stone, I flip to that file in my file cabinet, pulling out the patient's records. Her date of birth, phone number, contact information, and a small photograph of her are attached to her profile, along with the notes I made during our sessions.

On one of the pages is her hand-drawn sketch. Three arches, but these aren't red. She had used a dark brown marker, but it's the same symbol. Harmony, I think, but I can't place any of the information. Who was the leader of this cult?

Taking a leap, I ask Malcolm for his phone.

"Really?"

"Yes, I'm sorry. I just need to make a quick call."

"Don't apologize," he says, handing it over.

Using the contact information on the client profile, I call Becky. Surprisingly, she picks up on the fourth ring. "Hello?" She sounds confused. "Who is this?"

"Hi," I say. "We spoke a few years ago. My name's Willow Grace. I was helping you with your-"

She cuts me off. "Oh, Willow. I didn't recognize the number. I would've had your phone number saved."

"Oh, it's not my phone, but I wanted to talk to you."

"Okay, is everything all right? It's been a couple of years, but oh my gosh. I think of you so often. You truly saved my life."

"No, you saved yourself. You left a terrible place on your own with your own strength."

"You were always good at making me feel stronger than I was.That's one of the reasons I loved our session so much."

"Well, I was wondering if you could help me," I say. "Not to bring up your past trauma, but the place you joined, Harmony. Do you remember the name of the leader of that group?"

She clears her throat. "Yeah. It was Father Benjamin."

"Do you have a last name?"

"Benjamin Shaw. I have a picture of him. I could text it to you."

"That would be greatly appreciated. I think he may have rebuilt the cult closer in a new location," I tell her, "and I'm trying to make sense of it."

"Damn, well, I can text you a picture if you'd like."

"I appreciate it," I say. "So Father Benjamin Shaw, do you have any more information about him?"

"Not really, I haven't spoken to anyone since I left," she says. "But if you need any help, let me know."

"Thanks, but law enforcement are involved now."

"Good, if you can take that man down, a lot of people would be safer. I can't believe he started a group again using the same name."

"Old habits die hard," I remind her.

As soon as I hang up, there's a ping on Malcolm's phone. I open the message seeing the photograph of Father Benjamin Shaw. What a creep.

"Malcolm," I say. "I need to call Agent Holt."

"All right," he says. He pulls a card out of his wallet. "This is his contact information."

"Thank you."

I dial the number, and Holt picks up immediately.

"Hey, it's Willow. Where are you?"

"I'm following Moon."

"Is it going well?"

"Honestly, no. He left the main road, and it's impossible to follow him undetected on these rural roade. I've been driving in circles. I lost him a ways back."

"I'm sorry, but I have some news."

"Really? What?"

"I have a photograph of the cult leader."

"The cult leader? I didn't know we were dealing with a cult case."

"I found the symbol Megan had been drawing. I knew I had seen it before, and I was wracking my brain all night when I was in that cell. A few years back, I treated a patient, Becky Stone, and she had been in a group called Harmony. She drew the same image for me in our sessions. Anyway, when she left the cult, it's because it completely disbanded. I guess there was some big reason for tension and discord in the group. All that to say, it dismantled as far as she knew, but I don't think it really did. Megan was drawing the same symbol, and I think she's with him."

"The leader?"

"I mean, it's possible."

"That's true. And you have a name?"

"Yes, and a photo," I tell him. "I'll forward them to you."

He tells me he's pulling over, and I send him what I know. He checks his phone as we're talking. "Let me see if I can get a location on him. I'll call you back. All right?"

A few minutes later, Holt calls Malcolm's phone.

"Hello?" I answer it immediately.

"The information helped. We were able to locate him."

"That was fast."

"Yeah. Well, he's an idiot who has a van connected to an address."

"You think he's there? It could be a fake address."

"It could be, but it's only four miles away."

"From my house?"

"Yes," he confirms.

"Megan has been living that close to me all of this time?"

"It appears so."

"Are you going there now?"

"Hell yeah," he says. "It's time we take down this bastard and Moon too."

37 PAXTON HOLT

THE GRAY SKY is heavy with clouds, and as the rain begins to fall on my windshield, I curse under my breath. It's only going to make it more difficult to locate Moon and Benjamin Shaw.

Damn. I had inklings that something sinister was happening, but seven years ago when I was assigned the missing children's case, I never imagined they'd been abducted by a cult leader. Now it makes more sense. The way Megan was dressed, her fear, her inability to formulate words, not trusting police officers. I shake my head in regret realizing why she must have been so fearful of me, of all of us. Moon is connected to this cult; he has to be.

Jedd Jedd calls with Benjamin Shaw's last known address. It's difficult finding the long dirt road that leads to the compound, but according to my GPS, I've got it. To be honest, it's not unlike Willow Grace's long road to her cabin, only this is a dirt road, not gravel, and the road is windy, up and down a hill. Huge, thick pine trees surround the path, obscuring whatever lies beyond it.

When I try to call Jedd back, wanting him to have a read on my location, the call doesn't go through. The cell reception out here is spotty, just like it is at Willow's place, so I'm on my own. I know this is out of character, and not taking the precautions I should – but then I think of that little girl, of other girls like her – being kept at this compound and all reason is gone. I must act.

There are lights in the distance as I continue to drive down the road. The compound is up ahead, but I'm not going there in this vehicle. I pull off the road into the woods. Thankfully, my car is four-wheel drive and can handle the terrain.

I park, turning off the lights, shoving my keys in my pocket, and reach for a flashlight in my glove box. I zip up my raincoat along with the hood, bracing myself for the elements once I get out of the car. The flashlight is lowered to the ground. I don't want anyone to see me approach, but I also know time is of the essence. My biggest fear right now is that they have Megan, and they have plans for her.

Darkness settles in around me as I begin to approach on foot. A branch breaks under my foot, and I clench my fists in annoyance at myself. I've got to be more careful. I don't want anyone to see me until I have a better read on the situation.

As I get closer to the compound and the barbed wire fence that surrounds it, fear settles over me, just like the rain. This is not a single building; there are many houses.

This is not some small enterprise. Whatever this is, it's much more dangerous than I had imagined.

38 WILLOW GRACE

Soon after I get off the phone with Holt, he texts me the location of Benjamin Shaw.

I'm not sure why he wanted me to have this information. He's not clear, and when I try to send a text back, "Message failed." pops up.

I look out the window. "It's raining again."

Malcolm nods. "Yeah, it's going to get torrential. Did you make the call that you needed to?"

I nod. "Yes, I got a hold of Holt, and I have a location on Shaw."

Malcolm frowns. "Why do you need that?"

I hesitate. "Maybe it's better if I don't tell you everything. You are my lawyer, right?"

"I think that's the opposite of what you're supposed to do with your lawyer."

"Still, I don't think you want to be a part of this," I tell him, knowing I am hurting him. I don't have a choice. I need to go to Holt; I need to help find Megan.

I walk away from the living room back into my previously locked room. Inside, there is a small cupboard built into the wall. Inside is a fire box. I unlock it, pulling out a revolver. This one is more deadly, with more power. Not like the small pistol I had in my kitchen.

Malcolm is behind me. "What are you doing with that?"

"I told you not knowing would be better."

"Willow, I don't want you to make a mistake. You just got off the hook for a crime. You don't want to go down this road. Think of all you have to lose, like your job. You're going to be tenured soon. And what about your writing career? You have so much to live for."

"Yeah, well, so does Megan Talbot, and I need to go make sure that little girl is safe."

"Leave it to the authorities," Malcolm advises, stepping toward me. "Don't get involved, Willow."

"Why? Why do you care?"

"Because I care about you."

"Yeah, well, I'm not ready for that."

"You know I never meant for that to happen."

"It still happened." I pulled away from the situation, but a kiss still happened. The memory is still there.

"That was a long time ago, and that has no bearing on what I do right now."

"Let Agent Holt deal with bringing Megan home."

"Home? She doesn't have a home anymore. She doesn't have anyone. She's been living with some freaky cult for the last seven years, her mom died last night, and she's alone in the world."

"And it's your job to save her?""

"Well, the authorities haven't done a very good job of protecting her, have they? Maybe it's my time, my turn to help."

"You help a lot. You help your patients. You have so many clients, helping them through difficult, traumatic times."

"I know, but I'm helping people after the fact. I didn't get to save them."

Perhaps it's my way of trying to turn back the clock of my own life and heal my childhood wounds. No one saved me when I was a child, when I was being locked in a room, left for days as punishment for my crimes against my parents. Talking back. Not saying grace.

I can't let that happen to Megan. I shake my head, the gun in my hand.

"I don't have time to waste," I tell him. "Thanks for everything, but this next part I have to do alone."

I leave my cabin, Malcolm gaping at me as I leave in my car.

Fifteen minutes later, I'm driving down a dirt road headed toward a compound. Toward danger. Holt sent me his location, and I know I am the last person he should have sent it too—I am not in law enforcement – but part of me knows he needs me. Needs me in ways I don't entirely understand. And maybe we are acting without thinking, but at this moment, I don't care. I want to help.

I drive slowly, not wanting to draw attention to myself, and I turn my lights off. Before I do, though, I see Holt's car tucked in a cluster of trees.

Pulling in next to him, I cut the engine. His car is off. No one's inside. I jump out of my vehicle and walk around his, wondering if he's crouched down, not wanting to be caught. But he's not here. There's no sign of anyone.

It's dark now, and I don't have a flashlight. I don't even have a phone to use to help me on this path. But I don't care.

Now, my intuition is going to lead me.

39 MEGAN TALBOT

THE ROOM they've locked me in is small, like a closet. There's no light except for a tiny sliver at the bottom of the door. I can't try the knob to see if it's unlocked because they tied me to a chair with my hands behind my back and a strip of tape across my mouth.

I use my tongue between my lips trying to loosen the hold, but it's not possible. And even though it sounds weak, I've given up on getting the tape off my mouth.

Besides, what's the point? If I scream, I'll be hurt, punished even more severely than I already have been.

I should have done a better job of running away and not have stayed in the alley. I should have kept going, kept moving, then I wouldn't be here, caught again.

As I swallow back my fear, tears fill my eyes, and I blink them away telling myself to be brave, "Be brave, Megan. Be brave like Kevin wanted you to be."

Kevin was the bravest person I've ever known. My big brother was the best person in the world. He loved me and looked out for me. I can't believe he's gone.

I don't want to start sobbing back here in this closet, and I don't want my shoulders to shake. If they hear me, I will be in trouble. I have to stay strong, just like my brother.

The night we escaped, it was all because he planned it out. He knew where there was a break in the barbed wire fencing out behind the stables. He only knew it because a coyote had slipped through, and he'd watched Earl kill it, slit its throat with a knife.

Not sure why Kevin told me that story, except it was a warning. He said, "It's not safe here. We need to go. The people here are not good, they're not kind. If they're able to hurt animals, they'll be able to hurt us too."

I knew he was right, because in my heart I knew I'd been being hurt my whole life. For as far back as I could remember, I'd been put in rooms like this to pay my penance when I did things wrong, like not bowing my head deep enough for grace and not saying, "Thank you, Father," when I passed Father Benjamin.

The people who say they are my family have not protected me. The mother and father who I've been living with for the last seven years don't treat me like a daughter, rather they treat me like a servant.

I don't mind helping, I like to do my part, but I don't like the pain that comes with it sometimes when I make a mistake, when I'm not thinking things through, like Kevin, who's always one step ahead. Until he wasn't.

He told me we needed to escape during the elders' meeting. All the kids were supposed to be gathered to work on our chorus songs while the adults had a meeting. But Kevin took my hand, and he told me to run. We left, and it was so dark outside, and all I had with me was my dolly, which is ridiculous. Why did I think a doll would save me?

Earl must have seen us go because it wasn't long until he was following us, ready to hurt, to strike.

I assumed the worst thing he would do was drag us back to Father Benjamin where we would be punished. But that's not what he did.

It's probably because if Earl Dawson doesn't mind killing an animal, he doesn't mind killing a person either.

My ears perk up as I hear voices coming closer; I am both hopeful and scared. Do I want someone to open this door and let me out? I don't think so. The longer I stay in here, the longer I'm safe. And I'm not sure I'm ready to handle whatever comes next.

Father Benjamin is talking. "What were you thinking? You had one job, Moon, one job, to make sure that woman was the patsy, and now she's walking free. What kind of sheriff are you?"

"A loyal one," I hear Sheriff Moon reply. "I'm loyal to you, I have been for a decade. What more do you want me to do? How was I supposed to know she had a backup to her video camera on her phone?"

"You should have done better," I hear Earl Dawson say, but his voice seems small, and I realize he's a boy compared to these men.

"There's only one way to clean this up," Father Benjamin says.

"What's that?" Sheriff Moon asks, his voice gruff just like it always is when he is not making pretend faces and wanting people to like him. He's mean, and he likes to hurt people, just like Earl and Father Benjamin. All us girls, we're here to take their rage, and we're not allowed to talk about it.

"There's only one way for you to clean this up," Father Benjamin repeats. "You kill the girl, and you find someone to pin it on. It shouldn't be that hard, you're a goddamn sheriff."

"I can't, it's not possible. There's no way out."

Father Benjamin chuckles. "There's always a way out."

A second later, a gunshot blasts through the building, followed by a howl. I'd cover my mouth with my hands if either of them were free. I squeeze my eyes shut instead, scared.

"Be brave. Be brave. Be brave," I repeat, but how can you be brave when someone's just been shot? I don't even know who it was, Earl, Father Benjamin, or the Sheriff.

Seconds tick by, and then I hear Father Benjamin speak. "Earl, you clean up the mess you created, or you'll be next. Do you understand?"

"You want me to... You really want me to...?"

"Yes. Finish this off, finish it for good. We'll get rid of the girl, and no one will know she's been here. People will think she was lost in Tacoma forever. Do you understand?"

"But what about Sheriff Moon? What about..."

"You clean up that mess, I'll clean up this one."

I hold my breath as the lock on the door releases. It's pulled open ever so slowly, and Earl Dawson stands in the entrance, my brother's murderer.

His eyes are wild, frantic, searching mine with a menacing scowl. "Don't worry," he hisses. "It'll all be over soon."

40 PAXTON HOLT

Every step I take feels like I'm drawing attention to myself. I'm holding my breath, walking as carefully as possible. Keeping my body against the tree line to stay in the shadows. Thankfully, the rain is heavy, and it's masking my movements.

The last thing I need is to be detected before I can make a move. As I near the barbed wire fencing, I get a much clearer view of the compound.

This place is in the middle of nowhere, with no signs marking its existence. It looks like there are a dozen small buildings, presumably homes, and lighting along a trail path. Further away, there's a big barn, stables, and farming equipment. In the center of the buildings, there's a big square with an awning over some tables, I presume that's a gathering space of some sort.

I walk around the perimeter of the barbed wire fencing, wanting to find the entrance, and I do. There's a large gate with four guards standing at it, guns in hand, as if they're ready. As if they're preparing for something. I wasn't sure if Megan was here, but now I feel a pulsing inside of me, a certainty. They wouldn't be so alert if they didn't think there was potential for them to be caught.

Above the entrance, I see signage, and it startles me. It's the three arches, painted red, on a piece of wood, nailed to the fence. This is where Megan's been. This is where Kevin was all this time. Tucked in the middle of nowhere, in the woods.

I walk closer, a branch breaks underneath my foot, and the guards turn in my direction, toward the noise. I crouch low, not wanting to be found. One guard speaks. "It's probably just an animal, a raccoon or some shit. This is stupid. Why are the four of us out here anyway? No one cares about a little girl."

"Maybe not, but you want Father Benjamin to know you left the post?"

"Do we really need four people out here?"

"I don't know. What if someone's coming?" The guys are trying to plan, but they're failing at it pretty miserably. It sounds like the only person they take orders from is Benjamin Shaw. I want to know where Moon might be. I know he came here. And there's no sign of Megan, but I am certain she's arrived.

As I scan the compound, I finally see Earl Dawson's vehicle. That shithole truck is parked by one of the cabins. I feel vindicated; at least I'm in the right spot. A man steps from the shadows onto the porch of the house with the truck.

A cigarette illuminates his face, and I'm surprised to see it's Moon. He takes a long drag of his smoke before tossing it out and heading inside.

"Shit," I say. I need backup now. I try my cell; no luck. I keep trying Tamara, but the calls fail as I try to figure out my next move. Should I just leave altogether, go back to my car?

Before I can make a move, there's a crack of a twig behind me.

I spin and see Willow Grace.

Our eyes lock and there's a moment's pause as I register that she's here.

She really came. When I gave her that address, I don't know what I was expecting, but I think a part of me was hoping that she's as tough as she seems.

"You should go," I say, even though I don't want her to leave.

"No," she refused. "Besides, where's your backup?"

Whispering, I reply, "I'm not sure they got my location, cell coverage is shit out here."

"You're telling me, but if you don't have other backup, looks like I'm all you got."

She's beside me now. We're shoulder-to-shoulder, looking out at the compound. "We're going to have to make a move," I decide.

Before we do, we hear a gunshot.

41 MEGAN TALBOT

He moves closer to me, arms outstretched. I shake my head. "Ah, you're such a stupid girl," he says. "I always thought Kevin was an idiot for thinking you were so fucking great." He rips the tape off my mouth, hard. It stings. I know he grabbed skin. I want to bite him, hurt him. Instead, I say the truest thing I know. "Kevin was not stupid for loving me."

He chuckles, looking over his shoulder. Benjamin Shaw is there. Earl unties me from the chair, grabbing my body hard, dragging me. Benjamin Shaw shakes his head. "This is why we never leave the fold, child."

I see Moon slumped on the floor as Earl throws me over his shoulder and stalks through the small cabin. I've never seen a grown man curled up in a ball, moaning. The light from the cabin is on, and I see the blood pooling under his left side. The stain on the front of his shirt was darkest over where his heart would be. It's impossible to imagine the way his body would've fallen to the ground, and I try to push that thought away, but I can't. I was just a few feet away behind that locked door while a man was shot point blank.

It was just like the way it was when Kevin died. I was hiding in the shadows, watching it unfold, unable to say or do anything, because if I did, I knew Earl would kill me too.

Earl moves into the rainy night. It's cold and dark and tears fall from my eyes. They don't run down my cheeks, though, because I'm being jostled so much. Earl opens the door to his truck, shoving me into it.

I flail and kick my legs, hitting against his chest. "I hate you. I want to go. Let me go."

But the rain muffles my screams. No one hears me, and who would listen anyway? The women who live here, who are held captive just like me? The children who are scared for their lives, locked in closets to pay their penance?

None of the men here care. The only reason we're here at all is to serve them.

I kick at the door, but he slams it against me. "Shut up, you stupid girl."

I move my hand on the latch before he can lock the door, and I shove it open. It hits him against the shoulder. He's enraged by the blow and reaches for me, but I drop to the ground. He tries to grab my feet, but I roll under the old pickup truck.

He curses, dropping to his knees, "Get over here. You don't understand. Your time's run out, child."

"Don't call me a child! Don't talk to me! I'm not coming with you. You're not hurting me." I stay underneath the pickup truck, thinking if I stay here long enough, he'll give up.

But I should know better; Earl doesn't give up.

From underneath the pickup truck, I see two sets of feet approach. "Put your hands up, now." I scurry out from the other side of the truck, tiptoeing around the truck bed, watching with wonder as Agent Holt and Willow Grace tell him "to put his hands up."

Earl doesn't listen. He grabs the gun from the waistband of his pants as he stands. And just as he does, he sees me watching by the truck bed. He lunges for me before I can dart away.

I should have stayed under the truck, but I was so surprised to see people here to help me. Now Earl has me again. Squeezing me hard, his hands and fingers dig into the skin at my shoulders.

And then he points the gun at my head. I feel him. I smell him. The cool metallic of the barrel, the way his dirty hands pulse at the trigger. I hold my breath, terrified. My entire body shakes and trembles. And it makes me wish I would've spoken before, when I was at Willow's cabin and she was asking me those questions, or when I was in the interrogation room with Holt, and he was trying to get answers.

I should have told them everything. I should have spoken up and been brave. That's what Kevin wanted me to do. I wasn't brave then, but I will be brave now.

"No, don't," I cry, desperate to be anything besides a human shield.

Earl thinks holding me like this will keep him from being hurt, but that's not how it works.

"I'm going to kill her," he says.

"No, you're not." Holt levels his gun at Earl. I watch as he maneuvers ever so slightly, taking a confident aim. I cower low to the left, and he lifts his gun to my right. And it's like we're working together in this instant as he shoots and hits Earl in the shoulder.

Earl braces himself. I can feel the way his body grips the ground, his feet digging for holding, because he pulls the gun from my head and points it at Holt. "I've always hated cops," he says, before he pulls the trigger.

Holt is shot in the arm. Willow screams and so do I.

And Earl has fallen to the ground, same as Holt. Sirens blare in the distance. Finally, people are here to help.

I run to Willow and her waiting arms. She squeezes me tight. We look at the scene before us. Earl may have been strong for a moment, but the shot in his shoulder has caused him to fall to his knees. He's dropped his gun.

Willow grabs it, holding me under her arm, like a wing. She points Earl's gun right back at him. "You stay there, or I shoot."

Holt attempts to sit up from where he is lying in the dirt. "Damn," he says, "You really were the backup I needed."

They share a look I don't understand.

But then again, maybe I do. Because the way I feel for Willow is all soft, and all good, and that's the same as the look they share now.

42 WILLOW GRACE

A WEEK LATER, I'm back at work. Walking onto campus feels like everything that happened over the past seven days was a dream. I take that back. It was solidly a nightmare, taking me back to my past in ways I was not prepared for.

Taking down a cult was not a part of my fall lesson plans, but I guess it will add more validity to my lectures. The students are dying to know everything. There was an article in the Olympian Times over the weekend, which laid out some facts, and while I wasn't named, I was listed as a local professor of psychology at Conifer College.

My students put two and two together, which wasn't too difficult considering I'd been gone from work while this was all unfolding. Caroline is here in my office where I am putting some of my items back now that I am completely cleared for work.

"It's just so wild," she says. "I mean, talk about some real life experience!"

Little does she know. She thinks the closest thing I've been involved with in a cult is helping save Megan from Harmony, but that's far from the truth. I have spent way too many years living in the shadows at other people's mercy, but Caroline doesn't need to know all that.

She just needs to understand the basics of cult psychology so she can do her job better once she graduates. Maybe she'll be a new researcher or a professor. The sky's the limit for a student like her. She's bright and eager and smart as a whip.

"You should look into working for the FBI," I tell her.

"Really?" she asks.

"I mean it. You're bright, and you have an eye for detail. Maybe they could use an intern this summer."

"Well, that would be kind of cool. I never thought about looking into being an agent."

"What were you thinking you'd do after college?"

She shrugs. "I was mostly thinking about starting up a practice."

"That's always a good route, too. I'm excited to see what you decide to do, regardless, and if you want me to put in a good word with the agent I know at the Seattle office, I can."

Her eyes widen. "Wow, Professor Grace! That's really kind of you."

"My pleasure. So today," I tell her, "I was thinking we could hike up the cliffs."

"Really? It's a little ambitious."

"Sure," I say. "But it's not raining. The sun is out, and we're taking advantage of it."

She smiles. "Want me to post about it in the Google classroom?"

"That'd be awesome," I say. "See you in a few hours." She waves goodbye as Dean Clarence waves hello from the doorway.

The dean enters my office. "Willow,I wanted to come by and make sure you're doing all right."

"I'm fine,I'm happy to be back at work."

"And back on your trails."

I smile. "Yes, I know it's weird, but..." I shrug. "I'm a little weird."

“Not weird. Lots of people do things a little unorthodoxly here. Did you hear about the algebra teacher who took everyone out on a fishing expedition?”

"I don't even know how those things relate, but I'm not one to judge," I tell him.

He grins. “The thing is, Willow, I really want to offer you my deepest apologies. You've been through hell this last week and none of it was because of anything you had done. I wanted to believe you, but—”

“It's all right." I interrupt, "I understand. You have to do your due diligence. You have a college to protect and students to take care of. If there was any possibility that I had done something criminal, you made the right decision. The kids here need to be safe. All kids need to be safe."

The dean nods, apologizing again, before letting me know that he's happy I'm back all in one piece. Just as he's about to leave, there's another knock on the door, and I look over past the dean's shoulders seeing Agent Holt.

His arm is in a sling, but his eyes are bright.

"Hey, Willow" he says. "I'm Agent Holt." He introduces himself to the dean. Clarence leaves, and I am left alone with Holt. My heart-beat quickens.

"Looks like you are doing okay," I say. "I'm happy to see you're in one piece."

"Yeah. Were you worried?"

I shake my head. “Not even a little. Does it hurt?"

"The shot could have been a lot worse. It could have been my chest instead of my arm."

"I thought agents were supposed to be wearing bulletproof vests."

"They are in theory, but I wasn't exactly thinking I was going to a cult shoot-out that night."

"Fair enough," I say.

He chuckles. "You seem like you're happy?"

I nod. "I'm happy to be back at work."

"You love it?"

"I do, but I've been wondering about what happened at the department. Was Deputy Howie also involved?"

Holt shakes his head. "Moon was the only bad seed; he'd grown up in that cult. They'd been living in Eastern Washington before they regrouped here."

I nod, remembering that piece from my old client, Becky Stone. "Benjamin Shaw was arrested for his role in the abduction and murder. We found several other members who were taken into the group against their will. Thankfully, the FBI will handle the investigation against them and the return of those members to their old lives and helping them transition. Some of them were kids just like the Talbots. They were being used as laborers, and there was plenty of emotional abuse, too. That kid, Earl Dawson, is a prime example of that."

I nod. "Yeah. He's brainwashed beyond his own good. He killed Kevin and was willing to kill Megan. Just children." I pause. "Do you think he should go to prison for life?"

"It's complicated," Holt says.

I swallow. "It is. On one hand, yes, he did this heinous thing. On another, he had been primed to do it since he was a child."

Holt looks at me. Those sea blue eyes penetrating a part of me I wasn't expecting. I pull in a breath stepping back. He clears his throat. "You know what you just said about Earl's case being gray?"

I nod, "Yeah?"

Holt continues to speak. "The thing is, not everyone sees it like that. That's what I think makes you special."

"Special, huh?"

He nods. "Yeah. The world isn't so clear cut, is it?"

"I don't think so. I think maybe there's more good than there is bad. Just depends on how we look for it." Our eyes meet, and I have to look away, the intensity is so strong. "What's going to happen to Megan?"

"I heard talks about a few options. Her social worker, Lucy, is looking to find a suitable foster family for her."

"Really?" I shake my head. "So much transition. So much change. She needs something stable. The recovery assistance she's going to need is enormous."

"I'm scared the system's going to fail her," Holt says, reading my mind.

"Me too," I say softly.

"The trauma she's faced is deep and lasting."

"Maybe I could take her in," I say. "Until a permanent plan is made."

"You may have your hands full now for a while if you take Megan in," he says, "but I have a feeling the FBI is going to need your help again sometime soon." His gaze meets mine. He runs a hand over his smooth jaw. "And taking her in, even for a little while, is a big decision, Willow."

"I know, but what's the point of all of this? Of life? If we're not fighting to make the world a better place?"

Holt smiles. "So you don't think it's just about catching the bad guys?"

I shake my head. "No, I don't. I think life is about being fully alive, embracing all of it. The good, the bad, the beautiful."

Did you enjoy *Shadow of Grace*? Leave a review and tell us what you think!

https://www.amazon.com/dp/B0C37VYR21

CONDITION OF GRACE CHAPTER 1

AMY CARTER

People are quick to judge those with money, especially when you have lots of it. That's why I never lead with who my family is. The moment people learn my dad is Jackson Carter, things change. So, I keep it under wraps.

Being a part of the 1%, it's not something I'm proud of.

My father, on the other hand, finds money the only reason for living.

As a child, y life revolved around excess. Vacations in far-flung places, clothing that was top-of-the-line, and every Christmas it wasn't about the list you asked Santa for; it was shopping sprees with Daddy's credit card. Forget the fact a kid just wants their most wished for item wrapped under the tree.

My mom died when I was four. She was a philanthropist who used my father's money for good, and now that I'm grown, I have decided to carry on her legacy. It would be easier of course, if I had access to all my father's money right now, but most of it is locked up in a trust fund. He wants me to work for the family business part-time while I'm in college. He thinks I'm wasting my time at art school anyways. He wants me to take things more seriously since I'm the heir. But I want to use my free time to volunteer. Besides painting, it's my one true joy in life.

"Amy, did you find any new art supplies?" Sarah asks, tugging on my arm.

She's a nine-year-old girl who has been living at the shelter for the last few months. She moved in with her mom and younger brother after a domestic violence situation.

She's been through so much, so I do my best to brighten her day the best way I know how. She has an artistic streak that I want to encourage so I smuggle in craft supplies I know she'll love. Since I've been going to art school, it's easy for me to get extra paper and markers to bring to her at the shelter.

"Actually, Amy, I do." I've just arrived at the shelter and I haven't had time to take off my jacket or put away my bag. I open my tote that's resting on my shoulder and pull out the items I brought her. "There is a package of stickers in there too. Dogs and cats, which I thought you might like."

She squeals in excitement and turns to find her mom. "Look what Amy brought me! Thank you." She beams as she runs back to her brother. I laugh as I walked down the hall toward the volunteer room where I can stash my things. I see Doris, the woman who runs the shelter. She smiles warmly at me.

"Hey, Amy," she says. "I was thinking about you. Any interest in taking a few shifts over the weekend at the food bank?"

"Let me check my schedule," I tell her. I pull out my phone and open my calendar app. "I'm going to be working on a school project Saturday morning but I'm free the rest of the afternoon and Sunday too."

"You're a lifesaver. Kami and her husband John are sick, so they won't be able to make it in."

"It's really no problem," I tell her. "I just wish we could get some more people to volunteer. In Seattle there should be lots of corporate types who are free on the weekend."

Doris shrugs. "I think most of the people who are working for the man don't think about the people on the bottom."

I bite my bottom lip. She doesn't know who my father is. That's the sort of thing I keep on the down low. If she knew, she might look at me differently, and I don't want that. I have access to some money, but most of it is locked up in a trust fund. It's not like I can just throw hundreds of thousands of dollars into the food bank or the shelter. Not yet at least. One day, if I inherit my dad's company, Axon Integrated Solutions, ASI, a company that's at the forefront of a biotech breakthrough, I would be able to support the shelter.

It's partly why I have been considering caving in and doing what my dad wants. He wants me to work part-time for his company while I'm in school. And while I don't really care about biotech breakthroughs, I do care about using his money to help those who are less fortunate.

I spend the next few hours doing what I can at the shelter. Cleaning the bathroom, running laundry, and checking in with some of the kids living here to see if anybody has anything they need. While I don't have money to operate this entire facility, I do have enough extra cash to buy new socks or cute hairclips for some of the littlest residents. These kids find joy even in the smallest things. It's the least I can do to share what I have.

A few hours later, I tell Doris goodbye before grabbing my coat and purse. When I exit the shelter, it's gotten dark out. I pull out my phone and text my roommate Julie letting her know of the home soon and asking if she wants me to pick her up any food.

I slip my phone back into my pocket and scan the street and sidewalk. It's not the best neighborhood, and so much of Seattle is like this. Homeless camps are set up in the underpasses and corners. Buildings have been boarded up, and businesses have closed. It used to feel a lot safer here, and I try not to lean too far into fear, but the truth is I am a young woman, it's dark, and it's a big city.

My hyper-awareness is on even higher alert as I realize there is a man a few paces behind me. I look over my shoulder, wondering if he is someone I might know from the food bank, but I have never seen him before. He's wearing a dark hat and a black jacket. Still, as I continue to walk, I have a strange sense that he's right here on my heels. I quicken my pace.

My Tesla is just ahead, parked a few blocks from the shelter in a side alley, so no one notices what sort of car I drive. It was a high school graduation gift from my dad, and I couldn't exactly return it for something less flashy without causing him to get upset.

I pull my key fob from my purse and unlock it. Still, I look over my shoulder once more, exhaling as I do when I see no one is behind me. I am being ridiculous, assuming the worst. No one is here, and no one is following me.

As I move to pull open the driver's side door, someone grabs me from behind. I shriek as a hand tightens around my bicep.

"Let go of me," I shout.

"Shut up," a gravelly voice demands. Then a cloth is pressed to my mouth. I try to pull away, but as I resist him, I breathe in.

And within seconds, everything goes black.

CONDITION OF GRACE CHAPTER 2

WILLOW GRACE

Driving onto campus always puts me in a good mood. Today is no exception. The weather is crisp and getting cool, and while there's not quite frost in the air yet, I can feel it coming. As I park my car and walk toward the psych building where my office is located, I can't help but smile. It's been a long few weeks.

After wrapping things up with Harmony, the cult that was positioned in the town where I live of Olympia and watching the way my whole world got wrapped up in the case, I finally feel like I have closure.

Of course, the custody of Megan Talbot is where my head's been for days. After the cult dissolved and Megan was free, there was a short window of time when I thought I might become her guardian. But then, unexpectedly, after the case closed, an aunt who lives in Spokane contacted the police department. They had lost contact with Megan's mother several years earlier but had heard about the case on the news and wanted to claim Megan. They were family, and even though I wanted to have her in my life, I realize you don't always get what you want.

Still, the best thing for her is to be somewhere safe and secure, and the social workers in Spokane have given me assurances that she's well cared for.

As much as I would've loved to jump into the role of guardian, it might've been a bit too much to bite off at once.

It's not like I had a good example of parents growing up. And I'm not naïve enough to think that the way my life is set up, in such a remote and isolated way, would be a good fit for her anyways.

Maybe one day I will be a mom, but today I am going to focus on getting my job back.

Yes, getting my job back.

Because even though I was completely cleared of any wrongdoing and had, in fact assisted the FBI in closing the case with Harmony, Clarence, the Dean of the psychology department, sent me an email yesterday saying the president of the college is worried about their image and therefore pausing before they give me my job back.

When I get to my office, I see a note taped to my door. "Are you kidding me?" I groan. It's from Clarence, as if he didn't think I checked my email even though I replied to him immediately. I reread what he's written.

Willow, come to the president's office immediately. -Dean Clarence

Can he not just text like a normal person?

I roll my eyes and then stuff the note in my messenger bag. Then I begin winding back out of the building toward the president's office.

When I get there, I take a deep breath in and out. I'm not going to let anyone derail me. I worked hard enough on myself, and finding peace with my past so that I can focus on having a bright and beautiful future.

Yes, I know that sounds like a whole lot of unicorns and rainbows bullshit, but I have to cling to something, don't I? It's why I teach. It's why I write.

I can use my life experience as a cult survivor to help people understand the plight of being brainwashed under someone else's control. I could let my past keep me in the state of being a victim forever, but I choose light. I choose love.

Of course, most people don't think that I'm an optimist when they meet me. I look the part of a no-nonsense woman. I wear leather boots and basic Levi's jeans, fleece jackets, and I keep my hair in a simple braid. I'm not exactly screaming that I wear my heart on my sleeve. I'm pretty ordinary in terms of being a sort-of-granola-Pacific-Northwesterner.

And I'm not even close to being a hard ass. Once they get to know me, they realize I'm a softy, but I'm not. I have a rough exterior for a reason: I am not interested in getting hurt. The truth is, I'm scared.

So, I help in the way I know best. I teach. I use my experiences to help up-and-coming psychologists understand people who have been through trauma.

This is why it's so frustrating that the University president is more concerned about image than the welfare of the student body.

"I'm here to see President Orsen – –" I'm cut off.

The secretary smiles. "He will see you now; he's been expecting you."

I'm expecting a conversation in the very least. But when I enter Orsen's office, I see him sitting with Clarence.

Of course, he is.

"If there was a scheduled meeting, you could've let me know," I say, my tone announcing my annoyance.

"Professor Grace," President Orsen addresses me. "Glad you could finally join us.

I grit my teeth looking over at Clarence. "You didn't tell me there was a meeting I saw a note taped to my door. Why didn't you text or email about a time?"

"My mistake," he says, but I know he is full of shit. He wanted to set me up to look like a flake. "I really thought we had communicated about this," he says condescendingly. "Maybe things are slipping your mind?"

"Nothing is slipping my mind."

Clarence looks over at Orsen. Two men who both think they know everything.

I smile tightly. "Look, I've done nothing wrong. I simply helped the FBI find a local sheriff who was a murderer. How I'm connected to this is beyond me."

"You know enrollment is down," Orsen says. "The press we've had about everything going down in Olympia with the teenager being murdered and the cult, it's not good."

"You think since I work here, I'm going to mess up your enrollment? Maybe you should be doing something to drive a bigger student body. That's not my job. My job is to teach."

"I hear what you're saying, Willow, I do. The thing is," the president says. "Until we run this by the board, we're going to keep Professor Janet Albany running your classes."

"Why am I being punished?"

"This isn't a punishment. This is due process," the president tells me.

"So, I don't have a say in this at all?"

"You do have a say. You can choose your behavior as we move forward. However, until the temporary suspension has been lifted, you are on a paid leave of absence."

"This is ridiculous," I say, shaking my head in frustration.

"Well, you can bring that to the board," the president tells me.

Not wanting to get into this any further, I shake my head and leave the office, storming across campus. This is completely unjustifiable. This job is my life. I just lost the chance to parent Megan, and now the position that I've worked my whole life for is being threatened.

I march over to another building, knowing I need help.

And my good friend Malcolm Baldor is the help I need.

CONDITION OF GRACE CHAPTER 3

PAXTON HOLT

"The great news is Megan Talbot has been reunited with her aunt. That's the best-case scenario in a tragic situation." I offer a tight smile. Hoping that I've said enough.

"I really appreciate every extra bit of detail you've given the story," Veronica Young tells me. She's a journalist for the Seattle Collective, a magazine that covers everything happening in the city. And even though the Harmony case was central to Olympia, it's a hot story. A local cult that has been trafficking kids is no small thing.

Hell, I've been contacted by television show producers wanting a stab at the story for a new series on streaming services.

But God knows I'm not going to go down that road. An interview with a local reporter is torturous enough. Besides, the stuff that Megan and her brother Kevin went through was heartbreak. The last thing I'm interested in doing is sensationalizing their trauma.

"I assume you have enough?" I ask, wanting to get the hell out of this interview.

"I think so," Veronica says with a smile. She taps her phone, ending the recording. "You know, if you ever want to talk about things off the record, we could grab a drink or something?"

"Are you asking me out, or are you looking for details on the case?"

"Does it matter?" She gives me a flirtatious laugh.

"Actually, no."

She smiles brightly, but when I lift my eyebrow and shake my head, poorly concealing my annoyance, her smile fades.

"Okay, point taken," she says, rolling her eyes.

"I'm not trying to be rude. I'm just honest."

"Brutally honest," she says with a frown. "But whatever, it's not just you. It's every man these days. You all suck."

"I'm assuming that's off the record too?" I ask with a chuckle.

At that, her frown fades and she laughs, too.

"You need to be off the record," Veronica says. "I think most women are in consensus about this. Regardless, it was nice to meet you, I think."

"Will you email me when the piece comes out?" I ask her. I want to forward it to Willow. It's hard for me to come up with a reason to talk to her. It's been a few weeks since the case closed with Harmony, and I've been missing her. She was easy to talk to, but it's not just that. There was something about Willow that drew me to her. Now, I need a reason to see her again.

— —

When I return to the office, my buddy Jedd who sits one cubicle down from me, calls me over. He tells me the boss wants to see me.

"Really?"

Jedd shrugs. "Yeah, I guess you're still the popular one in the office."

"You know what it's about?" I ask, dropping my backpack into my chair and pulling my phone from my pocket to see if I have any missed calls or emails. Nothing from Willow.

"No idea, but if it's something cool, try to get me in on it okay?" he asks.

I chuckle, knowing he is a new kid on the block, and whatever my boss Tamara Rodriguez wants to see me about is probably not something she's wanting to loop him in on.

I head to Rodriguez's office and knock on her door a few times.

"Come in," she says.

She is sitting at her desk, looking as put together as ever. Her hair is pulled back in a tight bun. Her makeup is immaculate with dark red lipstick. That always makes a woman appear more powerful.

Not that anyone would question Tamara Rodriguez's power. She runs this unit, and she knows her shit. Everyone's intimidated by her, her husband included. She has two grown daughters who are off in college, and now that she has a bit more free time, she's more committed than ever to her job.

"Jed said you wanted to see me?"

"Yes," she says with a smile. "How was the interview?"

"As miserable as you'd assume."

She laughs. "God, Holt, you're always a drag. A lot of guys would think is pretty awesome to be interviewed by someone as gorgeous as Veronica Young."

"You know Veronica?"

"Of course, I know everybody in this town. She's pretty. You should ask her out."

"Why would I want to go out with her?"

"I don't know, maybe to get laid?

"I feel like that might be crossing some HR lines."

She laughs. "Okay, fine. I forget you're such a stickler for doing everything by the book."

At that, I roll my eyes. "You know that's not true."

"I know, which is why am teasing you, Holt. Listen, I need you."

At that, I lean in playfully. "You need me?"

She laughs. "Not like that. I need you on a missing persons case. You got the assignment."

Intrigued, I ask, "What's the deal?"

"The deal is you've been rewarded for finding Megan after she was missing for seven years. Now you find someone else who is missing. This one has only been a few days, though."

"I want to know everything," I say, ready to tackle a new project.

"I'm emailing you a file right now." There's a swoosh sound as she clicks the keys on her keyboard.

I pull out my phone and click on my email. I open the file she's just sent. I give a low whistle. "Amy Carter, the heir to the Axon Integrated Solutions fortune?"

"Yep, pretty high profile. It's going to be a task force operation. You're assigned to it. And will need to be working with a detective from the Seattle PD."

"Wow. Sounds big."

"It's huge. Her father, Jackson Carter, is a tech billionaire, and his little girl is gone."

"How little are we talking?"

Of course, I'll do my job, but dammit, I hate cases involving children.

"Oh, not little like Megan. She's twenty-one, a student at the Seattle Art Institute. And I guess she is the polar opposite of her father. She's all about giving back to the community."

I chuckle. If you read anything on Twitter you know her dad Jackson Carter is a grade-A asshole.

"There are local police involved from the Seattle department. But the FBI has been given the lead."

"I guess when a billionaire is missing, things move quickly."

Tamara nods. "Sad but true. The more money you have to throw at a situation, the more you get what you want."

"So where was Amy Carter last seen?" I ask Tamara.

"As I said, she gave back to the community. I guess she was working at the homeless shelter on 14th and Pacific before she was abducted. She never made it to her car, but it was left unlocked, and considering it's a Tesla, that's a surprise."

"And the last place she was seen was a shelter?" I clarify.

"As far as we know."

"Thanks for the assignment," I tell her. I know she's the reason I got it.

She shrugs, her eyes already back on her computer. "Don't let me down, Holt."

I grin, "I never have before."

WILLOW GRACE SERIES

Willow Grace FBI Thrillers

Shadow of Grace

Condition of Grace

Hunt for Grace

Time for Grace

Piece of Grace (coming soon)

ALSO BY WITHOUT WARRANT

More Thriller Series from Without Warrant Authors

Dana Gray Mysteries by C.J. Cross

Girl Left Behind

Girl on the Hill

Girl in the Grave

The Kenzie Gilmore Series by Biba Pearce

Afterburn

Dead Heat

Heatwave

Burnout

Deep Heat

Fever Pitch

Storm Surge (Coming Soon)

Willow Grace FBI Thrillers

Shadow of Grace

Condition of Grace

Hunt for Grace (Coming Soon)

Gia Santella Crime Thriller Series

by Kristi Belcamino

Vendetta

Vigilante

Vengeance

Black Widow

Day of the Dead

Border Line

Night Fall

Stone Cold

Cold as Death

Cold Blooded

Dark Shadows

Dark Vengeance

Dark Justice

Deadly Justice

Deadly Lies

Vigilante Crime Series by Kristi Belcamino

Blood & Roses

Blood & Fire

Blood & Bone

Blood & Tears

Queen of Spades Thrillers by Kristi Belcamino

Queen of Spades

The One-Eyed Jack

The Suicide King

The Ace of Clubs

The Joker

The Wild Card

High Stakes

Poker Face

Made in the USA
Middletown, DE
09 December 2023

45102513R00129